# “What brings yo[illegible] wa[illegible] dorm?” KC asked.



*Warren faced her and smiled. “I came over to ask you to Winter Formal.”*

*KC’s pulse went wild. She tried to maintain her cool composure, but her insides went crazy. “Actually, I—I already have a date,” KC blurted.*

*Warren looked right at her. “Break it. I know you have a chance at freshman princess. If you show up with me, there’s no way you’ll be overlooked. We’ll be the best-looking couple there.”*

*“But I haven’t said I’d go with you yet,” KC stammered.*

*“Yes, you have.” Warren leaned in and kissed her. Then he touched her chin and looked at her with his dazzling, photogenic face. “You said yes the first time you laid eyes on me.”*

*KC knew that he was right.*

**Don't miss these books in the exciting FRESHMAN DORM series**

*Freshman Dorm*
*Freshman Lies*
*Freshman Guys*
*Freshman Nights*
*Freshman Dreams*
*Freshman Games*
*Freshman Loves*
*Freshman Secrets*
*Freshman Schemes*
*Freshman Changes*
*Freshman Fling*
*Freshman Rivals*

And, coming soon . . .

*Freshman Flames*

# FRESHMAN GAMES

LINDA A. COONEY

HarperPaperbacks
*A Division of* HarperCollins*Publishers*

This is a work of fiction. The characters, incidents, and dialogues are products of the author's imagination and are not to be construed as real. Any resemblance to actual events or persons, living or dead, is entirely coincidental.

HarperPaperbacks *A Division of* HarperCollins*Publishers*
10 East 53rd Street, New York, N.Y. 10022



Cover art by Tony Greco

First HarperPaperbacks printing: February 1991

Printed in the United States of America

HarperPaperbacks and colophon are trademarks of HarperCollins*Publishers*

10 9 8 7 6 5 4 3

# One

he Coleridge Hall lobby bustled with activity. Art majors set up displays of pottery and painting. A flute player warmed up. Two theater-arts majors carted out an old, dried-up Christmas tree while flames crackled in the fireplace and a flutter of snow fell outside.

KC Angeletti yawned. It was early. They were all setting up for the Post-Christmas Clearance Craft Fair, a bargain-basement sale where all the Coleridge arts majors could get rid of their creative wares that hadn't been bought as Christmas presents. KC was one of the few non-Coleridge, non-creative-arts majors there, but she knew that her table would be among the most popular. She was selling the U of S Classic Calendar, a collection of photos of the best-looking students on the University of Springfield campus.

"I won't even need to lower the price," she reminded herself with a smile. The calendar had become so popular that KC and her business partners couldn't keep up with sales. She was eagerly awaiting a new printing that morning.

Meanwhile, she flipped through her single copy of the calendar and checked her watch. When she got to the model posing for December, she stopped and stared.

"Good morning, Warren Manning," KC whispered. Warren's hair was black and straight, cut so that one long lock fell diagonally across his forehead. His photo peered up at KC with sleepy, sapphire blue eyes. His jaw was square and his lips were parted in the most intimate of smiles.

KC chuckled, flipping the calendar's pages again. "Talk about saving the best for last. Ho ho ho." She giggled, then put a fingertip to her lips and looked around. "Okay," she told herself. "Enough. It isn't good business practice to lose your head."

KC didn't usually pay attention to guys, let alone stare at them. But guys didn't usually look like Warren Manning.

Still, that morning KC had a professional image to maintain. "Faith and Winnie, are you ever going to get here?" KC sighed as she wiped the dust from her tabletop and set down her copy of the calendar. Her two best friends, Faith Crowley and Winnie Gottlieb, were supposed to meet her and help with sales. KC was hoping that Faith's rich roommate, Lauren Turnbell-Smythe, might even pitch in and help, too. But she hadn't seen any of them at breakfast.

Faith and Lauren lived right upstairs in Coleridge Hall, but Faith, a theater-arts major, had probably gotten stalled by some dramatic inspiration. And just about anything could have kept Winnie, since she was late to nearly everything. KC, on the other hand, was always on time. She figured that promptness and success went hand in hand.

"And where are the rest of my calendars?" KC checked her watch again and prayed that her new stock of calendars would arrive before the craft fair officially got underway.

"Is that KC Angeletti?"

KC looked up at the sound of her name, hoping to see Faith or Winnie or someone delivering a load of calendars. But it was Kimberly, the pretty black dance major who lived next door to Faith in Coleridge.

"Oh, hi, Kimberly."

Kimberly glided through the maze of tables. She was wearing sweats, leg warmers, and a sweater with reindeer leaping across it. She was carrying a box of something that looked like hardened blobs of spaghetti.

"Hi!" Kimberly said cheerfully.

KC peered into the box that Kimberly was carrying. "What are those?"

Kimberly laughed. "Reject Christmas-tree ornaments. Gross, huh? A friend of mine made them. No one bought them before Christmas, and I don't think anybody will buy one now."

KC agreed. "They're certainly . . . unusual."

"You can say that again." Kimberly dangled one ornament by its string and made a face. "Can you imagine actually sticking this on your Christmas tree? You might as well hang up a five-day-old pizza."

"Maybe there's somebody on this campus who loves five-day-old pizza."

"I doubt it." Kimberly hopped up to sit on KC's table. She tugged at her leg warmers, then picked up KC's calendar. "But I bet about five hundred people here still want to buy your calendar."

"You think so?"

"I know so."

"Actually I'm hoping for sales of about five thousand." KC grinned. She was the marketing consultant on the Classic Calendar and would receive a percentage of the profits. She needed extra money badly, because her hippie parents, who ran a health-food restaurant back home, didn't have a penny to spare.

"Everybody in my hall's been talking about this calendar," Kimberly assured her. "I bought three copies before Christmas. My younger sisters loved them."

"Really?"

Kimberly nodded. "Your picture is incredible. You look like a professional model."

"Do you think so?" KC had originally gotten involved with the calendar because she'd been asked to pose. And she'd only agreed to model in order to get involved on a business level.

"Do *I* think so?" Kimberly scoffed. "Come on, KC. You look totally gorgeous. That picture of you is not to be believed."

"It's just a photo." KC wasn't sure yet what to

make of her photograph, although she had a heady sense that it might turn things around for her, that it might transform her from an ordinary freshman business major into someone sought after and important. During fall rush, KC had ruined her chance of joining the Beta Beta Beta sorority. But after word of her calendar had gotten out, there had already been several very friendly letters from sororities taped to her dorm-room door—including one from the Tri Betas.

"It's not just a photo," Kimberly said, opening the calendar. "It's art."

KC stared at her face above the month of March. There she was, her face taking up the whole page, all glossy lips, sculpted cheeks, perfect skin, and challenging gray eyes.

"I love how everyone is supposed to look like a classic movie star," Kimberly went on. "Was that your idea?"

KC shook her head. "Matthew Kallender thought up the whole thing."

"They're all great photos." Kimberly quickly flipped to the last page. She elbowed KC and let out a low, lusty laugh. "Who is Mr. December?"

KC leaned in and stared, too. "Warren Manning. He's supposed to look like Clark Gable."

"Talk about knockout."

"I know."

Kimberly flipped to July, where a gorgeous black guy, who happened to be student-body president, posed as Sidney Poitier. "Wow! What a hunk."

"I know."

Kimberly sighed.

"It was my idea to have half the models be guys," KC mentioned proudly.

"Good thinking." Kimberly pointed at Mr. July again and pretended to faint. "I wouldn't mind going to Winter Formal with him. I wouldn't mind going *anywhere* with him. I wouldn't mind just standing here for a few years and staring at him." Kimberly finally laughed and gave the calendar back to KC. "Oh well. Let me know when you get more copies in. I'll buy twelve."

With that Kimberly did a quick time step, then took her box of coagulated-spaghetti ornaments and went off to set up a table of her own.

"Let's hope I have at least twelve calendars to sell," KC muttered to herself as she rechecked the lobby for a sign of Faith, Winnie, or her calendars. Still, she wasn't as concerned about sales as she had been a few moments before. She smiled. She rocked back and forth on her patent-leather flats. If Kimberly thought that much of her photo, and all those sororities were impressed, who knew what the calendar could lead to?

When KC still couldn't find her friends, she let the calendar flop open to March again. She stared at her photograph, amazed at the confidence in her eyes, the perfection of her features, the smoothness of her skin.

"Too bad she's so ugly."

"Excuse me?" KC stammered.

"Who'd want to pay money to look at a face like that?"

"What?"

"Well, there's no accounting for taste. Here you are." A guy dropped a heavy carton a few inches from KC's hands.

KC quickly closed the pages of her calendar and took a step back.

"Here are three hundred copies." He ripped off a plastic cover, then took stacks out of the box and dropped them on the table. Each one landed with a loud *whack*. "Believe it or not, your picture's in every one. With all these calendars, you can stare at yourself until the cows come home."

"I wasn't staring at myself!" KC bristled. "I was just making sure that the new printing looks all right. I happen to be the marketing consultant on this project."

"And I happen to be the calendar's photographer." He leaned over and waved his hands right in front of her face. "Hello, KC. It's Peter."

KC stared.

"Peter Dvorsky. The man behind the lens. The eye of truth. Or consequences. Remember me?"

A light finally went on in KC's brain. "Oh. Right. Of course. Hi, Peter."

Peter kept unpacking. "Hi, KC."

During the calendar photo shoot there had been so many bright lights that KC had barely seen Peter's face. Besides, he wasn't someone who stood out in a crowd. His hair was blond but not golden, and his eyes were run-of-the-mill brown. He wore a white T-shirt, a faded denim jacket with a muted green scarf, and stonewashed jeans.

"It's about time you brought the calendars."

"Sorry, Your Highness. In case you hadn't noticed, it's snowing out. I had to look for something to cover the box with. I figured that soggy calendars might not be too appealing."

"Oh." KC looked out through the lobby picture windows. Light, lacy snow was still falling, and disappearing as soon as it hit the ground.

Peter unwound his scarf and let his photographer's bag slide off his shoulder. He blew on his hands. "So, I haven't talked to you since the calendar came out. What do you think of the photos?"

KC neatly spread the calendars over the table. "I think they look great."

"Thanks." Peter picked up his bag and sorted through some yellow film boxes.

KC opened a calendar to March and waited for a compliment in return.

Peter barely glanced at her photo. "You know, the light isn't quite right behind your hair," he finally commented. "But it's better than the way I lit Courtney Conner. Blondes are hard to light."

KC turned to Courtney's picture, which was opposite the month of June. Courtney was president of the Tri Betas. She was cool and beautiful and classy. "That's all you have to say about Courtney Conner? That blondes are hard to light?"

Peter shrugged and tossed the film boxes back in his bag. "I guess Courtney looks a little like Grace Kelly. Lighting and makeup can work wonders."

"What is that supposed to mean?"

Peter closed the calendar and shrugged. "Photography is illusion, KC. Just like a lot of things in life." He dropped the calendar on the table, then reached out and tousled KC's perfectly arranged curls.

KC flinched.

"Don't take it all so seriously." Peter smiled. "It's just a calendar. Half the people are going to buy it just so they can draw a mustache on your upper lip."

Peter slung his photographer's bag over his shoulder and, without another look back at KC, wove his way around the display tables and marched out the lobby door.

"Same to you, Peter Dvorsky," KC muttered, realizing that he had gotten to her. "Who are you, anyway?"

# Two

"I'm terribly sorry, Ms. Turnbell-Smythe."

"Sorry for what?"

"I'm afraid your overseas credit-card call will not go through."

"Why not?"

"Because your card has been canceled."

"What!"

"So sorry."

"But I didn't cancel it—"

"Thank you for using Mountain Telephone. And have a nice day."

*Buzzzzz.*

While the crafts fair was being set up in the

Coleridge lobby and the light snow continued to fall, Lauren Turnbell-Smythe stared at the phone in the upstairs hall. She couldn't believe what was happening. She had been trying to phone her mother in London and would have tried again collect, but now she was afraid her mother wouldn't even accept the call.

"Canceled!" Lauren gasped. First her mother had canceled the insurance on Lauren's brand-new BMW. And now this. What else was her mother going to cancel? Lauren's dorm contract? Her meal ticket? Her right to breathe?

"Lauren!" Faith suddenly called, leaning out of the dorm room they shared.

Lauren looked down the hall.

Faith was still in her nightclothes, a baggy T-shirt that had Western Drama Festival written across it. She held a rubber band between two fingers as she wove her long hair into a French braid. "Are you coming downstairs with me to help KC sell the calendars? I'm late. I lost track of time going over my *Alice in Wonderland* script."

"I don't know if I can go," Lauren answered. "I still have to print out my story for creative-writing class. And I have to make a few more calls."

"Is something wrong?"

Lauren shrugged. "Just this thing with my mom. It's worse than I thought."

"Anything I can do?"

"I don't think so."

"Okay. Let me know if I can help." Faith disappeared into their room again.

Lauren stared back at the phone. What if her mother had canceled every single credit card she'd ever given to Lauren? Lauren hugged her middle and tried to calm herself. Then she dug into her expensive leather purse, opened her wallet, and pulled out a rectangle of gold plastic.

"American Express," answered a polite voice after Lauren had punched in a new set of numbers.

"Hello," Lauren said, keeping her fingers crossed. She gave the man her account number. "I'd like to know if there have been any changes in my account recently."

"I'll check. One moment, please."

Lauren waited.

The man came back on. "I'm sorry, Ms. Turnbell-Smythe, but that account is no longer active."

"It isn't?"

"I'm afraid not. Please destroy your card."

Lauren's heart sank. "Thank you." She hung up, then forced herself to check her other accounts, starting with Saks Fifth Avenue, Visa Gold, and MasterCard. After those calls, Lauren decided to save her voice and the little change she had left. Her mother was nothing if not thorough. She had obviously cut off every outlet for money that Lauren could possibly have used to support herself.

"Thanks a lot, Mom," Lauren grumbled.

Faith popped out of their room again, this time wearing a denim jumper and cowboy boots. Her fringed suede jacket and her book bag were slung over her shoulder. "Lauren, I'd better go," she said. "Have you seen Winnie?"

Lauren shook her head.

Faith sighed. "Knowing Winnie, she probably forgot. Well, I'd better get downstairs anyway. You know how KC hates to be kept waiting."

"I know."

"Are you sure you don't want to come?"

"Not right now."

"Okay." Faith threw open the door to the stairwell and began to hurry down. "See you in Western Civ."

Lauren waved goodbye, then stared at the telephone again. *Maybe I* should *go down to the crafts fair,* she thought. *I could set up a table and sell off my designer luggage and cashmere sweaters, my pearls, my CDs, my computer, and my camel's-hair coat.*

Lauren leaned her forehead against the telephone. What a nasty trick her mother had played on her. After an upbringing of privilege and wealth, her mother was suddenly pulling the rug out from under her. Lauren didn't know anything about money. She had rarely carried cash and had never had a checking account, since she'd used her credit cards for everything. Nor had she ever seen the bills. She wouldn't begin to know how to organize a tag sale.

"Well, being broke is better than being tortured by the Tri Betas," Lauren said out loud.

That was the only notion that cheered her. Her mother had insisted that if Lauren was going to attend a state university in the West, she had to join the exclusive Tri Beta sorority. But the Tri Beta sisters had thought Lauren was a shy, chubby misfit. They'd invited her to pledge only because of her parents' money. And Lauren had hated every moment she'd spent in their elegant, exclusive house.

So Lauren had gone on a campaign to find her place at U of S and make the Tri Betas kick her out. She'd traded her prim woolens and sensible shoes for mukluks and drab parachute pants. She'd left her contact lenses in her drawer and dug out her old wire-rimmed glasses. She'd taken part in a campus demonstration, hung out with streetwise Dash Ramirez, and worked on a newspaper article that exposed a dangerous fraternity prank. And just when Lauren thought she had won, when the Tri Betas had finally banished her and she'd felt purposeful and free, her mother had made good on her threat, cutting Lauren off at the pocketbook.

Lauren indulged in another moment of hopelessness and gloom until she heard footsteps thumping up the stairs. When the stairwell door was flung open, a small, shapely girl burst out, bouncing as if she were getting ready for a boxing match.

It was Winnie Gottlieb.

"Lauren. Oh good. Oh wow," Winnie chattered, spotting Lauren right away and bounding down the hall. "I've been looking all over for you."

"Have you?"

"I definitely have." Winnie panted and pulled at her short hair. Her dangling earrings, which were shaped like Fred Flintstone and Barney Rubble, swung from side to side. "And here I am. Late again. I overslept."

Lauren nodded.

"I didn't actually oversleep," Winnie explained. "See, I was up early, or up late, depending on how you look at it, since I didn't go to sleep at all last night. But then I fell asleep instead of going to breakfast this morning and it was really hard to wake up again."

Lauren rubbed her eyes.

Barely pausing for breath, Winnie went on. "See, there was this party in my dorm last night —of course, there's always a party in my dorm— but Josh and I partied at this one." Winnie giggled. "I was in such a totally great mood that I didn't mind being up all night. I didn't think I would ever need sleep again. I saw the sun come up this morning and even sat down and studied for a couple of hours, but then I thought about you and your BMW and since I had all this extra time, I decided to call the insurance people and check on what was happening."

"Winnie, slow down," Lauren said as she felt her own heart begin to race. Before she knew that her mother was on the rampage against her, she had loaned Winnie her BMW. And Winnie had crashed it—the day after Lauren's mother had canceled the insurance policy. "What about my BMW and the insurance?"

"I don't want to slow down," Winnie admitted. "Because if I do, I'm afraid I'll lose my nerve and won't tell you what I found out."

"What are you talking about?"

Winnie finally stood still. Even in her pink tights, purple ski sweater, Flintstone earrings, and fake-leopard-fur boots, she suddenly seemed subdued.

"Winnie?"

"Okay." Winnie cleared her throat. "I called the All Safe insurance people again this morning, because I still feel totally and completely weird about smashing up your car, even though I know it wasn't my fault." She paused. "I asked the insurance woman what she had found out about the guy who ran into me."

"What did she say?"

Winnie bit her lip. "She told me that he doesn't have any insurance."

Lauren was confused.

"So I asked her what that meant."

Lauren was starting to dread hearing the end of Winnie's story. "And what did the insurance woman say?"

"Well, um, she said that since no one had any

insurance at the time of the accident, you could try and sue the guy who hit me, but she doubted he had any money. So you might as well just pay to fix the car on your own. Or take a loss and sell it the way it is."

Lauren felt as if she had just been bathed in ice. She knew that her mother was going to do everything she could to force her to drop out of U of S and enroll in some stuffy private school back East. Lauren's one hope had been to sell her BMW and live off that money for as long as she could.

"I'm sorry to be the one to bring bad news," Winnie said, looking truly pained. "I hate bad news, just as a general principle. I'm so sorry. If I could take the whole mess back, you know I would."

"I know," Lauren said, trying to convince herself that she could hang tough. "It wasn't your fault. I'll figure it out."

Winnie nodded. She gave Lauren a hug, then turned away.

Lauren stood there until Winnie went back downstairs to help KC. She didn't know what she was going to do. She only knew that if she wimped out now, it was all over for her.

* * *

"So then I had to go and tell Lauren the bad news about her BMW. I mean, she took it really well and all, but what a drag for her. I was totally bummed to find out that the guy who hit me wasn't insured."

"Winnie, do you have to talk about this right now? It's not exactly good for sales."

"Relax, KC. The calendars are selling themselves. Anyway, this morning, before I called the insurance place, I was in the best mood of my entire life. Josh and I had the greatest time last night, and it wasn't even some heavy romantic thing. I mean, there were moments that were heavy and romantic and wonderful and all that, but mostly we talked nonstop—"

"You mean, *you* talked nonstop," KC interrupted.

Winnie grinned. "We hung out in the dorm and then at four in the morning we hitched a ride in the back of this guy's pickup to the top of Wimer Mountain. We sat there with our arms around each other and watched the sun rise."

KC shrugged.

Winnie had a dreamy expression on her face. "Of course I'll probably snore through my History of Russia class, but I think it was the best night of my entire life. I'm going to ask Josh to

Winter Formal, even though I don't usually go to corny events like that. But Josh is so great, and our relationship is so great, that even something as weird as Winter Formal will be great, too. What do you think, Faith?"

"Me?" Faith stood between Winnie and KC, counting out change and handing out calendars. Between Winnie's desire to chatter and KC's desire to stand there exuding beauty as a form of advertising, Faith was the one doing the work. That wasn't unusual. What was unusual was that Faith wasn't really paying attention to her friends. She was thinking about the production of *Alice in Wonderland* that she was directing as an independent-study project. In a little over a week, her cast would do two performances, which would be attended by Faith's independent-study advisor and professors from the theater-arts department. As the performance dates drew closer, Faith's head was filled with thoughts about blocking and sound effects, light cues, costumes, and line readings.

"How can you say Winter Formal is weird?" KC said to Winnie. "From what I've heard, it's the biggest social event on campus." KC paused to smile and wave at someone she recognized.

"All the sorority and fraternity members go to Winter Formal."

Winnie rolled her eyes. "KC, I can't believe you're talking about sororities again. I thought you were through with that bozo stuff."

KC tensed. "And I thought you were through with Travis."

Winnie took a moment to respond. "I am," she finally insisted. "It's not my fault he hasn't left town yet."

"Does Josh know that Travis is still around?" KC asked.

"He doesn't know yet," Winnie admitted. "But he will. I'll tell him. Soon." She turned away from KC and neatened a stack of calendars. "Faith, you think that's okay, don't you, that I haven't told Josh about Travis yet?"

For once Faith didn't jump in and play referee, making sure that their old trio was still getting along. KC had good reason to question Winnie. After all, Winnie's old boyfriend from the summer, Travis Bennett, had suddenly appeared and was still in town, while her new boyfriend, Josh Gaffey, was under the impression that Travis had gone. But Faith sensed that KC's irritation wasn't really over Winnie's lack of truthfulness, but over Winnie's glowing happiness with Josh. KC might be the glamorous freshman on campus, but, unlike Winnie, she wasn't in love. She didn't even have a date for Winter Formal.

Still, Faith didn't comment on her friends' motives. She didn't tell Winnie to be truthful, or insist that KC keep her head. For once, Faith preferred to hand out calendars and think about the color of Alice's apron and whether the White Rabbit should scamper or hop.

"Who's that?" Winnie gasped, grabbing the edge of the table and letting her mouth fall open.

KC's mouth fell open, too.

Faith stared. A tall, dark-haired young man was walking up to their table. He wore a heavy sweater that matched his pleated wool slacks. He wasn't just good-looking, he was stylish and extraordinarily handsome. Faith recognized him instantly from the calendar.

"Oh my God, it's Warren Manning," KC blurted.

"Mr. December." Winnie giggled.

"He's even more gorgeous in person than he is in his picture," Faith whispered.

Warren came up to the table and offered KC a brilliant, paper-white smile. "Hello, ladies. How are sales?"

"Even better than we expected," KC managed. "And how are you?"

"Terrific."

Faith was amazed. When things got hot, KC seemed to get even cooler than usual. Faith didn't have time to think about guys right now, but she could never have chatted casually with Warren. Even madly-in-love Winnie stood there with her mouth open.

Warren, however, wasn't interested in Faith or Winnie. His eyes were on KC. He extended a hand to shake. "You're KC Angeletti. We met briefly during the photo shoot."

"Did we?"

"I'm Warren Manning."

KC nodded, as if she'd really needed a reminder.

Warren still held KC's hand. "I guess you're not only the beauty behind this, you're the brains, too."

KC stood taller, even more composed. "I guess so."

Shoppers nudged Warren, trying to get to the table to buy more calendars. He shifted and leaned toward KC. "I admired your photo, and when I saw you here, I came by to say hello."

"Did you?"

He smiled and acknowledged the crowd. "But I guess this isn't a great place to get acquainted. Why don't you give me your phone number? I'd like to get together sometime."

KC pretended to consider his suggestion for a moment. Finally, with Faith and Winnie staring like idiots, she wrote her number on a sales receipt and handed it to him. "There you are. Maybe we can get together and talk about the calendar."

"Among other things." Warren looked at the number, then stuck it in his pocket. He winked at KC. "Thanks. I'll give you a call sometime."

"You do that."

"I will."

KC maintained her cool composure until Warren had made his way back through the crowd and disappeared. As soon as he was gone, she faced Faith and Winnie.

For the first time that morning, the trio was perfectly in tune. At the exact same moment, Faith, KC, and Winnie put their hands to their faces, came together in a huddle, and screamed.

# Three

he light snow fell for the next two days. The weather was cold and wet, and it seemed as if half the people in Winnie's dorm were coming down with colds.

*Cough, cough. Hack, hack.*

*Poor Melissa,* thought Winnie.

Even Melissa McDormand, Winnie's roommate, the pre-med term-paper machine and track star, was lying in bed, a forest of tissue balls around her. Melissa's nose was pink, her freckles looked washed out, and her red hair was droopy.

"Mel, I'm going down to Josh's room," Winnie said. She stuck a few books in her carpetbag and tried to clean up a little. "Do you need anything? I could walk to the drugstore. Actually, it's getting so muddy out, I could probably slide there."

Melissa slowly rubbed her eyes. She groaned. "No thanks. I'm fine. I'll get up in a few minutes. I've got so much to do."

Winnie looked out their window. It was no longer snowing, but the sky was gray and moisture clung to the glass. "Melissa, you're not fine. Believe it or not, you are *not* about to go out and set a new track record today. You are not even going to ace another biology test. It's cold season. And you have a cold."

Melissa sneezed. Then she flopped back on her pillow. "I guess I do. I feel terrible. I hate to miss track practice, though."

"It's inhuman to make people run around in circles in weather like this." Winnie flexed her biceps. "Even I, the obsessive exerciser, am taking a few days off."

Winnie was about to open their door to leave when she realized that someone was standing on the other side, pushing his way in. He had blond curls, wore a Gore-Tex parka, and carried a hefty backpack. It was Brooks Baldwin, Melissa's new boyfriend.

"Hi, Mr. Brooks," Winnie said. "I'm glad you're here. I was feeling guilty about leaving Melissa all alone."

Melissa sat up, making a tiny effort to neaten her hair and straighten her T-shirt. A huge cough erupted from her.

Brooks hovered and took Melissa's hand. "How bad do you feel?"

Melissa tried to smile. "I'm okay."

"I brought you some things." Brooks began emptying items from his backpack and placing them on the edge of Melissa's bed. There was a quart of orange juice, vitamins, tea bags, a hot pot, and a large thermos. "Chicken soup," he said, pointing to the thermos.

"Brooks, this is weird," Melissa cried. "I don't need all this. I'm fine. Really."

Brooks looked a little hurt.

Melissa put her hands over her face and laughed. "I mean, it's great. It's wonderful. You're wonderful. Thanks."

"You're welcome." Brooks brushed Melissa's bangs away from her eyes, then sat back and gazed at her.

Winnie laughed. "Well, since the doctor has arrived, I guess I'll be on my way." Winnie waited for a response, but Brooks and Melissa were too busy sighing at each other.

Winnie walked out. In the hall she dodged two basketball jocks, who were singing along with a stereo and crushing beer cans. She thought about Melissa and Brooks. Brooks had been Faith's high-school sweetheart, so it was still fairly mind-boggling to see him going gaga over study-grind Melissa instead. And yet, Winnie told herself, that's what freshman year seemed to be about—surprises, the unexpected, and new experiences.

Winnie had had a few new experiences of her own. She'd had some of them the summer before, when she'd gone to Europe after high-school graduation and had met Travis Bennett. She and Travis had carried on a hot and heavy romance before Travis had left Paris to travel by himself. And then, a few weeks ago, just when she'd thought that Travis had forgotten her forever and she would never hear from him again, he'd contacted her and shown up in Springfield. Unfortunately, by that time Winnie had met an even more fabulous guy—Josh Gaffey—and for a short time she'd tried to juggle both guys, which had resulted in her crashing Lauren's car and nearly ruining things with Josh.

The biggest surprise of all, though, was that in the end Winnie *hadn't* ruined things with Josh. After so many misunderstandings and close calls, she and Josh had worked things out. They were finally together and it felt so good that Winnie walked around with a goofy smile pasted on her face. She'd never felt like this before. In the past, she'd been dumped, she'd been wild, she'd been infatuated and crazy and horrendously depressed. But she'd never been in love.

Winnie floated down the hall.

*Knock knock, rap rap, thump, drumroll, thump.*

She played a rhythm on Josh's door. Josh also lived in Forest Hall, on the same floor as Winnie.

"Who is it?" Josh called. "It had better be somebody important. We're in the middle of a world-class computer-game tournament."

"It's me," Winnie called back. "Open up, you insane techno-nerd."

"Winnie!"

Winnie heard Josh jump up and race to the door.

The door swung open and Josh grinned at her. "Well, why didn't you say it was you in the first place?"

"It's me."

"Hi, you."

"Hi, you, too."

For a moment they just smiled at each other like two love-struck twelve-year-olds. Winnie felt as if she could stand in the doorway forever, as long as she could look at Josh's long hair, his lively eyes, the single earring he always wore, and the quirky smile on his face. He had on a green T-shirt with a big bleach spot on one shoulder and sweats that were worn through on one knee. Winnie thought they were the most beautiful clothes in the world.

The next thing Winnie knew, she had dropped her carpetbag and was embracing Josh, her arms around his neck and his around her shoulders. They held each other for a moment, then started to laugh as they jokingly planted furious kisses all over each others' face.

Meanwhile, Mikoto, Josh's roommate, sat at Josh's computer skillfully manipulating the joystick. "You two are out of control," Mikoto commented, not turning to look at them.

"Mikoto doesn't like to be disturbed. He takes his computer games very seriously," Josh joked.

Mikoto pounded on the keyboard, then shook his head and cursed.

Josh picked a slipper off the floor and, without

glancing back at Mikoto, tossed it over his shoulder. The slipper landed on top of the computer.

"Interference!" Mikoto objected.

Winnie hugged Josh once more and stepped into the room. "That's my middle name."

"Hi, Winnie," Mikoto said.

Winnie patted his arm. Mikoto was a Japanese-American freshman who favored designer polo shirts and, like Melissa, was a pre-med.

"What are you doing?" Winnie asked.

"Josh was showing me this game program he worked on with his computer TA," Mikoto answered. "It has creature-eating Hostess Twinkies and Darth Vader–type guys who use corn dogs instead of swords."

Winnie looked at Josh. "Really?"

Josh smiled.

"And for this you need a college education?"

Josh lurched forward to handle the joystick while Mikoto narrated the game as if he were a sports announcer. The corn dogs and the Twinkies were going at it. Josh handed the joystick to Winnie, who tried to keep up the fight until she got wiped out.

"Oh well," Winnie sighed, leaning back against Josh while he slid his arms around her waist. "I got an A on my paper for my film class—which

I wrote in an all-nighter—but I get an F at Twinkies versus the corn dogs."

"No one's perfect." Josh played with Winnie's spiky hair, then planted a kiss on top of her head.

Mikoto shrugged and stood up. "Well, thrilling as that was, I guess I still have to do my mundane reading for class today. Computer games may come and go, but chemistry lives forever." He started to forage through his backpack.

Josh dug his chin into Winnie's neck. "I have reading to do, too. I've got to get through another chapter before English lit this afternoon."

"I'll go," Winnie offered, pulling away from him and picking up her bag.

"You don't have to." Josh came after her and took her hand. "Why don't you stay here and read, too?"

Again their eyes locked and they stood there smiling like fools.

"Okay," Winnie decided. She pulled her Western Civ text out of her bag.

The three of them settled into study mode. Mikoto sat at his desk while Winnie flipped to the next assigned chapter of her Western Civ textbook and Josh got out the book he was reading for English lit. Winnie and Josh stretched out on his bed, snuggling, legs intertwined as they began to read.

Winnie felt the softness of Josh's hair and the motion of his breathing. She was astounded at how good it felt just to hang out and study together, not worrying about whether Josh liked her or if she was coming on too strong.

That made her wonder about Travis. Their relationship had changed since Europe. Winnie no longer wanted to be wild and carefree, and she didn't want to just pick up and leave Springfield to follow Travis to L.A. He was planning to move there to start his singing career. So when Winnie had told Josh that Travis had left town and was out of her life, she thought she was telling him the truth. How was she to know that Travis would change his mind at the last minute and hang around after all? And how was she supposed to go back to Josh now and tell him that Travis was still in town?

Winnie went back to her book until Mikoto packed up some notes and a small tape recorder and left for class. Winnie snuggled closer to Josh. She wondered if it was time to be brave and bring up the news about Travis.

"Josh."

"Hm?"

"I need to talk to you about something."

Josh closed his book and sat up quickly, ready to listen to her. "What?"

Winnie was taken aback. She hadn't expected that kind of attention. "Well, it's nothing major. You can keep looking at your book."

"I'm done. What is it?"

Winnie sat up, too. Josh was looking at her with such affection that she couldn't bring herself to mention something as weird as the fact that her old boyfriend was still hanging around. "Winter Formal," she said instead, grabbing Josh's stomach and trying to tickle him. "It's next Friday night."

Josh tickled back. "Winter what?"

"Winter Formal." Winnie giggled. "You know. Corny corsages. Food that looks like what they serve you on an airplane."

Josh nodded. "Bad music. Tacky decorations. Waiting to see who gets to be freshman prince and princess and senior king and queen. It's a bizarre custom. Related to senior prom."

At the same time they yelled out, *"Let's go!"*

They laughed and then Josh pretended to be very serious. "Isn't it going to be held at the Springfield Mountain Inn?"

"It is."

"Ever been there? It's full of tourists, swinging singles, and lounge-lizard acts."

"How do you know?"

"I hang out there every weekend."

They laughed again.

"Actually, my parents stayed there when we came to visit the campus during my senior year of high school," Josh confessed. He kissed Winnie's neck. "Does this mean I get to see you in a dress that looks like a pink paper napkin and high heels that make you trip?"

"Absolutely."

"Okay. I'll rent a tux," Josh said. "And patent-leather shoes."

"No you won't," countered Winnie. "I won't be seen with a guy wearing one of those plastic-looking, phony rented tuxes."

"So what am I supposed to go in?"

"Well, I kind of like the idea of plaid pants, myself. And maybe a straw golf hat."

"Well, then, you have to wear something nerdy, too. Like a pocket protector and a calculator on your dress."

"What I wear," Winnie boasted, "will be a surprise."

"Let's make the whole thing a surprise," Josh said. "Let's dress as weird as we want, then meet by the indoor pool that's in the middle of the hotel complex."

"Yes!" Winnie clapped her hands. "We can pretend it's a blind date."

Josh nodded. "That way, if we're dressed too weird to even get past the ticket takers, we can sneak in. The room the dance will be in opens onto the pool."

Winnie grinned. "Josh Gaffey, you have a devious mind."

He looked right at her. "That must be why I'm in love with you."

Winnie almost couldn't breathe for a moment. She felt faint and giddy and shy and peaceful and out of control at the same time.

"I love you," she whispered before she knew she'd even had the nerve to say it. Then she looked up into Josh's face to see if saying it had been okay.

He was still smiling, still gazing at her, still listening with all of his heart. "You, too," he said in a surprisingly shy voice.

For the first time that afternoon, neither of them seemed to know what to say. They kissed instead.

Winnie picked up her carpetbag, and Josh

packed up his leather jacket and his books. They slowly walked out of his room.

Winnie floated back to her own room with a goofy smile on her face again. She hadn't told Josh about Travis, but she told herself that it hadn't been the right time. Every single second that she'd spent in Josh's room had been perfect. Winter Formal would be perfect. Why ruin it all with something as unimportant as the news that Travis Bennett was still in town?

# Four

In the middle of the Tri Beta living room, across a silver tray containing the cakes and scones that made up high tea, KC and Courtney Conner were sitting face to face.

"Sugar?" asked Courtney, the Grace Kelly look-alike and Tri Beta president.

KC offered a cool smile. "Please."

"One lump or two?"

"Three." KC's parents may have owned a health-food restaurant, but that didn't stop her from being as big a sugar junkie as most every other college freshman.

"Cake?"

"No thank you," KC decided, even though she could have eaten five pieces. She was tall enough so that she didn't have to watch her weight carefully. Still, she didn't want to give the impression of being totally undisciplined.

"I'm glad you could come over on such short notice," Courtney said, folding her hands over the red wool skirt she wore with a lacy blouse and short black velvet jacket. Her blond hair fell gracefully over her shoulders and her voice was as smooth and dark as deep water.

"I just finished a research paper for my business class, so I have some free time." KC didn't add that she had two more papers to finish before the end of the semester, which was only two weeks away, and that she only took the call on the hall phone because she hoped it was Warren Manning. When she'd discovered that it was Courtney, however, she hadn't been disappointed. The notion of Courtney wooing her as a potential pledge was almost as intoxicating as the thought of Warren wooing her for a date.

"Well, I'm glad that you could make time for me. I know how busy this time of year can be, between writing papers and getting ready for Winter Formal." Courtney reached for one tiny sliver of cake. "But I've felt so strange about the way things ended after fall rush. And I've been wanting to talk to you about it."

"You have?" KC managed to stay cool, even though her temperature had just risen. When she'd first arrived at U of S she'd wanted to be a Tri Beta so badly she'd ached for it. Except for her bohemian parents and lack of funds, she'd known she was Tri Beta material. The Tri Betas had known it, too. But when Lauren had been humiliated during a rush prank, KC had dumped an entire tray of drinks on Tri Beta sister Marielle Danner in an impulsive act of revenge. After that, the notion of KC pledging the Tri Betas was out of the question. And since that time, KC had gone back and forth about how much she still wanted to be a member of their house.

But now that KC looked at Courtney across the tea table, she no longer had any doubt. During her first semester as a freshman KC had been up and down. First she'd been embarrassed by her parents and her friends, then she'd been grateful for her parents and her friends. The only thing she knew now was that there had been lots of mistakes during fall rush, but the Tri Beta sorority was still where she belonged.

"I just wanted you to know that even though fall rush didn't work out, there's another rush this spring," Courtney explained. "I've always felt that you would be an ideal member of this house, KC. And I think so still."

KC sipped her tea. Courtney *had* been loyal to her all along, which KC appreciated. "Thank you."

"That's the main reason I called you," Courtney went on. "To make sure that you know there's still a place for you here. Fall rush had some unpleasant surprises for all of us, and I'd like to make sure that everything goes smooth as silk this next time around."

"That's fine with me."

"Good." Courtney smiled. Then she stared at KC, completely composed, even though it was obvious that she didn't know what to say next. "So tell me about your research paper," she finally suggested. "I remember you telling me that you are a business major."

"I am," KC said, ready to launch into familiar territory. When it came to her talent for business, she felt a blooming sense of confidence. "I did my paper on the U of S Classic Calendar."

"How wonderful! I really think that calendar turned out beautifully. I'm awfully glad you included me in it." Courtney put a manicured finger to her lips. "But I'm interrupting you. I'm sorry. Please go on about your paper."

"All right." KC shifted in the overstuffed chair. "I explained how we went into the calendar venture with as little capital outlay as possible. I'm the marketing consultant, but even I have to wait for my fee, which is a percentage of the sales. The photographer, a sophomore named Peter Dvorsky, is being paid that way, too. Do you remember him?"

Courtney looked blank.

"Of course you don't," KC blurted, wondering why she'd even brought Peter up. She couldn't imagine why Peter Dvorsky was on her mind. "Anyway, we sold very well at the Christmas Crafts Fair."

"Congratulations." Courtney gave KC a big smile, then suddenly turned away as if she was distracted by something or someone in the kitchen.

KC turned, too, and saw a flash of glossy, dark hair, slender limbs, and expensive clothes.

"Marielle," Courtney called with a slightly condescending tone. "You remember KC, don't you? Come in and say hello."

Marielle Danner froze in the kitchen doorway. She was trying to smile, but even her turned-up nose looked droopy. She'd been caught trying to spy and she knew it.

"Hello, KC," Marielle said curtly.

"Hi, Marielle." Seeing Marielle again after so long made KC's stomach lurch.

"I'm just on my way over to the ODT house to see my boyfriend," Marielle said, slipping back into the kitchen. "Sorry to intrude. Bye-bye."

"Goodbye, Marielle."

"Bye," KC whispered. She could hear the faint jangle of Marielle's charm bracelet as Marielle tiptoed out.

After Marielle was gone, Courtney folded her hands and sat up, signaling that KC's tea time was coming to an end. KC responded by sitting up also and putting her tea cup and saucer back on the silver tray.

"Don't worry," Courtney assured her. "Everything will go just fine this time." She stood up and gestured toward the front door.

KC picked up her blazer and scarf and accompanied Courtney across the living room.

"I'm glad to hear that you feel so good about your paper," Courtney said as she escorted KC, "because you know that you have to keep up a good grade average to be a member of our house. How do you think you'll do this semester?"

"Excuse me?"

"I'm sure you'll do very well."

They were stalled in the doorway with KC nodding and Courtney waiting for an answer. KC was doing well in business class, but she was worried about her other classes. She had needed money and had lost valuable study time looking for a part-time job. The calendar would eventually save her from financial difficulties, but it had taken even more time from her studies. Unlike Winnie, KC had never been one to make it on cramming and all-nighters.

"I'm doing fine," KC lied. "We just had an extra exam in Western Civ, but I'm sure my grade will be high."

"I'm sure you will, too." Courtney opened the front door. It was cold and damp out. The shrubs looked waterlogged and the lawns were soggy. "And I'm also sure I'll see you at Winter Formal next week. I think every girl in our house is going. I was hoping that one of our pledges would be picked for freshman princess, but after all the fuss everyone is making over your calendar, I'm beginning to think that you might win freshman princess instead."

"Me!" KC's heart stopped for a moment. Freshman princess was a huge deal. Being freshman princess was like being a celebrity. KC wanted to jump for joy. Then she remembered one small detail. The court was selected at the formal—and she might not be there. So far, she didn't even have a date.

"That's kind of you to say so," KC said, forcing herself to appear calm. "Who knows what will happen? We'll see."

"Yes, we will." Courtney leaned out of the doorway and patted KC's arm. "Thanks again for coming over."

"You're welcome. Thank you for the tea."

"You're very welcome. If you have any questions about spring rush, or about anything at all, please feel free to call me. Otherwise, I'll see you at Winter Formal."

"See you then." KC pulled on her gloves while Courtney stood in the doorway, waving. She managed to maintain her cool all the way to the corner of University and Sixth. But just before she left Sorority Row and walked back onto campus, KC groaned and let her face fall.

"Winter Formal," she muttered. "I'd better find a fabulous date, and I'd better find him fast."

"Thanks for coming along, Faith."

"No problem, Lauren."

"This is all kind of new for me."

"Don't worry. It's really not that big a deal."

Lauren took a deep breath. She and Faith were sitting in a small reception area outside the personnel office of the Springfield Mountain Inn. The room was furnished with high-tech mirrors, leather sofas, ferns, and posters of skiers flying down steep mountains. Like the rest of the inn, the waiting area for potential employees was a combination ski resort and swinging-singles bar and grill.

Lauren cleared her throat. Her voice felt stuck, her palms were moist, and her stomach felt as if it were bouncing around. "It's a big deal for me. Anyway, I'm glad you're with me."

Faith barely lifted her head from her clipboard. "I had to come downtown anyway to get some last-minute music for *Alice in Wonderland.* As soon as we're done here, I'll stop at the record store."

"Okay."

Faith looked up with an intense expression. "I was thinking of using a combination of rock and classical music for the opening scene, going from one to the other, to set up the feeling of reality versus illusion. Do you think that makes sense?"

"Sure." Lauren fidgeted. "Do you think I look okay?"

"Mm." Faith nodded. "You look good."

"KC said I should dress conservatively." Lauren stared down at her pale beige wool skirt and matching blazer, clothes she hadn't worn since leaving the Tri Beta sorority. She'd even put her contact lenses back in and set her hair. She felt as if she were in disguise. "KC says you should always look neat and understated when you're applying for a job."

Faith lifted her head and really looked at Lauren. She patted Lauren's wrist. "Don't worry." She pushed up the sleeves of her own thick, sloppy sweater. "I wish KC could have come with us. She's applied for a lot more jobs than I have. But she wanted to go over to the Tri Beta house to have tea with Courtney."

"Yeah." Lauren tried to smile. "It's weird, isn't it? All I wanted was to get out of the Tri Betas, and all KC seems to want now is to get in."

"It *is* weird, if you ask me," Faith agreed. She went back to her clipboard.

As grateful as Lauren was for Faith's company, she was beginning to wish that she'd also included Winnie. She was about to apply for her first job ever and she needed support! But Faith was so preoccupied now with her drama production that Lauren felt as if she were living in a single room. Lauren understood that *Alice in Wonderland* was a big deal, that it was premiering soon, and that very few theater-arts majors got permission to direct a production their freshman year. But she still wished that Faith had a little more energy left for her roommate.

Lauren bit a nail, then stared at a bulletin board that listed upcoming Springfield Mountain Inn special events. There was a singles' jamboree along with a divorced parents' club meeting and the U of S Winter Formal, which was taking place in the Powder Ballroom. Lauren didn't linger on the special-events notices, however, because she was much more interested in the sign next to it, the one that said, "Help wanted. Housekeepers, groundskeepers, bartenders, and disk jockey."

"Maybe I could apply for the job as a disk jockey in their disco," Lauren said, half joking, half wishing that she could really be considered for that position. When she'd thought about getting a job before this, she'd always glamorized working. But now that she was being forced to earn a wage, she realized that she didn't know what was in store for her.

"Have you figured out how much money you need to make in order to stay in school?" Faith asked.

Lauren looked down at her application form and shuddered. Her work-experience record was a virtual blank. KC had advised her to make up a history of work experience, but Lauren didn't have it in her to lie. She put down a few charity volunteer jobs and her experience at the newspaper. "Winnie and Josh tried to help me figure it out on his computer, after they went with me to sell what was left of my car. I only got seven thousand dollars for it."

Faith finally rubbed her eyes and put her clipboard away. "That sounds like a lot of money."

"Not to me," Lauren admitted. "Not when I have to pay my own dorm fee and meal ticket for next semester, plus out-of-state tuition. I think it'll cover all my basic expenses, but I'll still need to earn money for books and extras." Lauren shrugged. "I can easily live without a fancy car and expensive clothes. But I don't like not knowing whether I can afford to stay in school."

"Don't worry," Faith said, trying to be comforting. "It'll work out."

"I hope so."

The two of them sat for a while. Faith went

back to her notes while Lauren hummed and fidgeted and waited for someone to come out of the office and call her in.

"It's funny to think of having the Winter Formal here," Lauren said, trying to think about something other than her job interview.

"Is there any chance that you might go with Dash?"

The teeny bit of confidence that Lauren was trying to muster disappeared. Dash Ramirez was the most extraordinary person Lauren had ever met. He was funny and smart and streetwise. He worked on the campus newspaper and was involved in campus politics, and, most amazing of all, for a while he had been interested in Lauren. But that had ended when Lauren had been taken for a sucker by Christopher Hammond, a handsome, seductive fraternity jerk. Dash had always been a little suspicious of Lauren's upbringing and wealth, and seeing her with Christopher had turned the tide. Lauren had almost no experience with men, but even she could tell that Dash would probably never speak to her again.

"Ms. Turnbell-Smith?"

The voice broke into Lauren's thoughts like a hacksaw. She flinched, then froze as she saw a middle-aged man with molded hair, wearing a blue leisure suit. He looked back and forth between Faith and Lauren.

"Oh. That's me," Lauren blurted, clutching her application and scrambling to her feet. "Smythe. Turnbell-Smythe."

"Come on in, Ms. Turret-Smythe."

Lauren gave one last look to Faith, then followed the man into his office.

"I'm Mr. Zackis," he said, sitting on the edge of his desk and motioning her into a low armchair. His office was decorated like a smaller version of the waiting room. Little ferns sat next to his desk and there was a poster that said, Springfield Mountain Inn Is for Lovers.

"Nice to meet you," Lauren whispered.

He smiled. "It looks like you're my last interview of the day. We had quite a crowd earlier. We need to add fifteen new employees for the rest of the ski season."

Lauren sat quietly as Mr. Zackis looked over her application. When he looked back up with a skeptical expression, she expected to be sent right back out the door.

"You haven't had too much work experience, have you?"

"No." Lauren remembered KC's advice about

selling herself and keeping the ball rolling, but she couldn't think of another word to say.

His smile didn't fade. "Well, if you can show up on time and work hard, I think we can use you. Can you do that?"

"I think so."

He grinned. "Then the job is yours."

Lauren was so overjoyed that for a moment she stood there, hands together, letting out a little cry.

"Really!" she finally said, shocked and excited. "You can really give me a part-time job? You don't know how important this is to me. Thank you."

"You're welcome."

"What will I do?" Lauren asked.

He wrote something on her application. "I still need a housekeeper for weekend nights."

"That sounds fine."

"Good." He stood up and shook her hand.

Lauren started to leave, then turned back. "Um, what exactly are a housekeeper's responsibilities?"

He was already marking her in on his schedule. "Housekeeping tasks. You know, cleaning rooms, making beds, scrubbing toilets, emptying trash cans. You'll do fine. I'll call you and let you know your hours. Gladys Baker, the head maid, will show you what to do on your first day. Welcome aboard."

Lauren froze for a moment, staring at his plain, smiling face. When she'd looked at the word *housekeeper* she'd thought of the woman who used to run her family's house back in New York. Mrs. Bergstrom had attended to house-guests, made pots of cocoa, and tended a lovely flower garden. Lauren had seen herself doing all those tasks with energy and good cheer.

What Lauren hadn't imagined when she'd applied at the Springfield Mountain Inn was that she was going to end up working as a maid.

# Five

"Papers," KC grumbled from across the room that Friday night. "I've always hated writing papers."

"It's not exactly a fun way to spend a Friday night, is it?" said Faith. "But if I'm going to get this Western Civ paper in on time and still hold two dress rehearsals of *Alice in Wonderland* this weekend, I'd better work on it right now."

KC started to put pen to paper, then lifted her head again. "Do you know that I have two papers due the same day next week? And both professors mark you down half a grade for every day you turn your paper in late. I think it's a conspiracy."

Faith smiled. "I think so, too."

Winnie barely paid attention. Her thoughts were totally focused on her paper about Peter the Great. KC and Faith's voices were merely background noise, as was the occasional clacking of Faith's electronic typewriter and the screechy violin that someone was practicing down the hall.

The three of them were in Faith and Lauren's room having what Winnie called "a marathon paper-writing party." Faith sat at her desk, reading, thinking, and typing in successive bursts. KC was using Lauren's desk, but she hadn't gotten past her first page. Winnie, meanwhile, was sprawled on the floor, limbs spread, surrounded by a landslide of paper. She was blowing bubbles of purple gum and scribbling nonstop.

"Where's Lauren?" asked KC. She neatened her notes, her library books, and her indexed box of three-by-five cards.

"She's working." Faith bobbed up to peer into her typewriter and check the ribbon. "It's her first night as a maid at the Springfield Mountain Inn. She'll work Saturday and Sunday nights, too."

"What a drag." KC stared out the window at the lights casting long shadows across the walkways between the dorm complexes. It looked like it had begun to drizzle.

"KC, write some more," Winnie suddenly ordered. She glanced up to check Faith's alarm clock. "I'm telling you, this is the only way to nail a paper. You do your research, then set the clock for two hours, start writing and don't stop until the alarm goes off."

"Winnie," KC objected.

"Just write, KC! We only have four minutes more." Winnie blew a huge bubble, scribbled, and flipped over yet another page on her yellow pad.

KC got up from the desk chair and began to pace. "This is not the only way to write a paper, Winnie. As a matter of fact, I'm beginning to think that this is a total waste of time. I can't just turn my thoughts on and off like a faucet. Ready . . . set . . . write. I need to think and outline and carefully compose."

"If I did that," Winnie laughed, "I'd never turn in anything."

"I don't know how you do turn in anything," KC grumbled, "or how it ever makes sense, considering how fast you write it."

Winnie finally closed her pad and put her pen away. Her hands were dotted with ink. "I wouldn't be so critical if I were you, KC. I did all my reading beforehand and I'll write one more draft after this. If I remember correctly, I had a better average than you in high school, so I must have been doing something right."

"Yeah," KC scoffed. "You took the right classes. The easy ones."

"I did not!"

"Come on, you two," Faith said, playing referee. "I'd like to use these last four minutes to finish this paragraph, if you don't mind."

"Sorry." Winnie put her pad aside and began doing stomach crunches.

KC frowned and paced.

Winnie watched KC's high heels clomp back and forth and wondered why KC was in such a snit. During orientation week KC had suddenly decided that Winnie was an embarrassment and that the only people who had any value or class were the members of the Tri Beta sorority. Since Winnie couldn't think of anything she'd done to reignite KC's anger, she could only assume that the same thing was going on now. KC was once again idolizing the sorority sisters, and in contrast, her old friend Winnie seemed like a flake.

The problem was, however, that Winnie didn't feel like such a flake anymore. She still had wild impulses and moments of terrifying insecurity. The whole mess with Travis and Josh was a perfect example of how far over the edge she still could throw herself. But she wasn't going to carry on with two guys anymore. She was going down to the Beanery that very night to see Travis after his singing gig at the coffeehouse. She was going to tell Travis that everything was over between them and that she wanted him to leave town.

Winnie wondered if that was the reason that KC was irritated with her, because she'd been hesitant and a little flakey about Travis. But what was Winnie supposed to have done? It wasn't her fault that Travis wanted to stick around. And she was so relieved and happy about the way things were working out with Josh that she didn't want to deal with Travis anymore. She was hoping that Travis would fade away on his own.

*Beep beep beep beep!*

Faith's alarm finally went off and Faith exchanged her term paper for her *Alice in Wonderland* script. Winnie began gathering her papers into a messy pile and stuffing them and the yellow pad into her carpetbag.

"Where are you going?" KC asked pointedly.

"I'm going to the Beanery to set things

straight with Travis. Do you mind?" Winnie held up her bag. "See, I wrote for two hours and now I can go out without guilt."

KC didn't seem to be impressed. If anything, she looked even more annoyed. "You're going to see Travis now? It's almost midnight, Winnie."

"So? Travis sings at the Beanery until one."

"But if it's midnight now, how late will it be when you get back to the dorm? Don't you have your Western Civ. paper to do this weekend, too?"

"Yes, I do, KC. Who are you, my mother? I thought Faith usually played the mother role in this trio."

Faith didn't look up.

"Winnie, I don't believe you," KC muttered.

"Why?" Winnie demanded. "What's the big deal, KC? Why are you being such a jerk to me all of a sudden?"

"I'm not being a jerk," KC said defensively, coming over and standing with her hands on her hips. "I just can't believe that you still act like this even though we're in college."

"Don't worry about me, KC. I always seem to get along," Winnie argued.

"No, you don't," KC tossed back. "You always seem to mess up. And that's just what you're going to do with Josh if you don't get it together." KC stomped back over to Lauren's desk and began collecting her things. "Winter Formal or no Winter Formal!"

There was a stunned silence. Even Faith lifted her head and frowned.

"What does Winter Formal have to do with it?" Winnie asked. "Winter Formal isn't for a whole week."

"I don't know." KC was flustered. "I just mean —well, have you told Josh that Travis is still in town?"

"I think . . . I guess . . . well, Josh has figured it out," Winnie lied.

"And what about Travis?" KC pointed out. "Why does he think you've cooled toward him? You probably told him that you wanted time to think or had to write your term papers. You probably strung him along so he thinks he still has a chance. I doubt you told him that you were madly in love with someone else."

"Why are you picking on me all of a sudden?" Winnie exploded. She looked over at Faith, who was still hunched over her script as if she were cramming for her SATs. "Faith, why don't you take my side?"

"Hm? What?" Faith finally said.

Winnie slung her carpetbag over her shoulder. "Forget it. See you guys later. I've got to go."

Faith gave a spacey wave. "Bye."

KC glared and shook her head.

Winnie quickly walked down the Coleridge stairs and out into the cold, dark night. She'd been in such a great mood. Josh was great. Classes were great. Winter Formal was going to be great. Even her papers were turning out great. But even with all those great things going on, KC had managed to bring her down.

"I'm bummed," Winnie mumbled, sidestepping a puddle on the dark, soggy green and making a U-turn. "I think I'll get a half-dozen candy bars and go back to my room. I don't feel like going over to the Beanery anymore. I can go talk to Travis another time."

"Be careful when you take down the star, Marielle."

"Yes, Courtney."

"And make sure the ornaments are all wrapped in tissue paper."

"Yes, Courtney."

"And whatever you do, don't set the tree near the fireplace. The needles are so dry now that there's a terrible risk of fire."

*No, Courtney. Of course not, Courtney. Whatever you say, Courtney.*

Over in the Tri Beta sorority house, Marielle Danner was helping take down the sisterhood's Christmas tree. Marielle was trying to be cooperative and careful, but she was feeling so hot that she could have set the living room on fire all by herself.

"I'm glad that everyone else went to sleep," Courtney said, stifling a yawn. She sat down on a little stool and coiled strings of colored lights.

"Oh?" Marielle questioned.

"I wanted to talk to you, Marielle. Alone."

*Goody, goody,* Marielle thought. She was all too aware that Courtney was beautiful and refined, popular and smart. She was also aware that Courtney had absolute power over her as long as she wanted to remain a Tri Beta. And Marielle wanted to remain a Tri Beta for a very long time. "What about?"

Courtney put the lights in a box and pulled a newspaper clipping out of her pocket. "Have you seen this?"

"Seen what?" Marielle asked in mock innocence, even though she knew exactly what Courtney was referring to.

"This is an article that was in today's *U of S*

*Weekly Journal,*" Courtney said, her usual honey voice becoming even darker. "It's the exposé Lauren Turnbell-Smythe wrote. Apparently some guys from the Omega Delta Tau house forced one of their pledges to get horribly drunk. Then they made him take off his clothes and they stuffed him in a car trunk. Did you know they were involved in hazing?"

Marielle hesitated. Of course she had known. Her boyfriend, ODT member Mark Geisslinger, was one of the guys who had pulled the prank. "No."

Courtney gave her a cool, disbelieving stare. "My point is, Marielle, that it could look like we asked Lauren to quit because we objected to her article. You told me this article would be false, but it's not. I don't object to what Lauren wrote. I think that kind of hazing is wrong, too."

"We asked Lauren to quit," Marielle argued evasively, "because she was pathetic and wasn't showing up to required events and because we never should have invited her to pledge in the first place!"

Courtney stood up. "I don't like your attitude, Marielle. It was the decision of the whole house to invite Lauren to join us. Lauren Turnbell-Smythe is bright. She's a talented writer and journalist and she happens to be a lovely person. And I want to know why you took it upon yourself to disregard all that and force her out."

"Oh, Courtney, please," Marielle barked, her anger finally bursting loose. "The only reason you regret losing Lauren is because the alumnae board gave you hell for it."

"The board was upset to lose Lauren's mother's donations, but that's not what this is about, Marielle." Courtney sat down again. Her perfect, pale complexion had turned pink. "Enough about Lauren. She'll never come back. We've lost her and it's over and done with." She put Lauren's article back in her pocket. "But KC Angeletti is another story. Marielle, I want KC Angeletti to pledge this house after spring rush and I don't want you to get in the way."

Marielle wanted to throw up. Lauren was easy to write off, but KC was clever, uppity, and gorgeous. KC had insulted both Marielle and Mark in the crudest way when she'd poured a tray of drinks on them during fall rush. Marielle would never forgive her. First Marielle had had to sit by while KC became a campus celebrity because of her dumb calendar. And now she was going to have to sit by while KC was invited back into the Tri Betas. The thought made Marielle want to tear down the old Christmas tree and throw it right at Courtney.

"I know you don't like KC," Courtney went on.

"Why don't you just call her by her real name?" Marielle smirked. "Kahia Cayanne."

"I'll call KC by any name I like and you'll just have to deal with it," Courtney shot back.

Marielle glared.

"Because if you get in KC's way this time, your own future as a Tri Beta will be in serious jeopardy. Is that understood, Marielle?"

*I understand all right,* Marielle thought. "Yes, Courtney."

"Good." Courtney packed up the last of the ornaments, then marched straight up the stairs. "Good night, Marielle."

*I understand plenty,* Marielle thought after Courtney was gone. *I understand more than you know.*

Marielle understood that she would have to change her tactics. She would have to get back at KC without Courtney knowing about it. Because, short of losing her Tri Beta sisterhood, Marielle was ready to risk anything to see Kahia Cayanne Angeletti take a very big fall.

By the following night, the walls of KC's single room were closing in on her. When KC had started at U of S she hadn't wanted to clutter her dorm room with a single decoration or souvenir from home. She'd had no postcards taped above her desk, no photos of old friends tacked to her door, no stuffed animals on her window sill or pennants on her wall.

Since that time, however, KC had pasted up a few mementos, which she now realized had been a mistake. If she'd wanted distraction she could have lived in a coed party dorm, like Winnie. If she'd wanted to be homey, she could have plastered every surface of her dorm room with mementos, like Faith.

"Now my room looks like every other freshman dorm room on this campus," KC decided.

She got up from her desk and took down a photo of her dad standing in front of his organic vegetable garden. She tore down another of her, Winnie, and Faith making faces on the night of their high-school graduation. Finally she sneezed.

"And I'm coming down with a common cold, like every other stupid freshman."

KC flopped back in her chair and tried to console herself. If she'd wanted to be like every other freshman, she wouldn't have chosen Langston House, her all-girl, twenty-four-hour-study dorm. If she were stupid, she wouldn't have already been involved in two successful business ventures. And if she were common, Courtney Conner wouldn't have asked her to come over and talk about rushing the Tri Betas again in the spring.

But if she was so extraordinary, then why didn't she have a date for Winter Formal? Why hadn't Warren Manning called? Why was she suddenly picking on one of her best friends? And why couldn't she even write her paper for Western Civ?

"The first few pages still aren't right!" KC balled up another sheet of paper and threw it in the trash. She'd done a ton of research on her topic, the fall of the Roman empire, and she'd written three outlines and scores of notes on three-by-five cards. The result was that she was running out of time and still couldn't figure out how to organize her thoughts.

"Maybe it's just a form of writer's block," she told herself. "I should go talk to Lauren about it. She'll know what to do. As long as I don't take any more study advice from Winnie."

KC opened her neat drawers and pulled out a sweatshirt. For once she didn't want to think about the way she looked. She didn't want to think about Winnie, either. It was starting to drive her crazy that Winnie, the all-time flake when it came to guys, had a date with a terrific person like Josh for Winter Formal. And it drove KC even crazier that Winnie could goof off, then cram all night or write a term paper in a set amount of time, and probably still pull an A.

KC sneezed again and grabbed her keys.

She was almost out the door when she caught a glimpse of herself in the mirror. She froze. Her eyes were puffy. Her nose was red. She wasn't wearing any makeup and her hair needed washing.

"I look terrible."

So many people had been coming up to KC lately, telling her how beautiful she looked in the U of S calendar, that KC felt she could never leave her room now unless her hair was done, her clothes all matched, and her makeup was perfect. She knew that her appearance in the calendar was the sole reason for Courtney's renewed interest in her. Plus, she kept thinking that she was going to run into Warren Manning again, and she didn't want to look anything less than spectacular when she did.

"Well, I'm only going over to Coleridge Hall tonight," KC said, pulling up the hood of her sweatshirt and grabbing an old plastic rain poncho that had been her mom's. "There's no way I'm going to run into Warren Manning around the dorms. It's too dark out for anyone to really see me anyway."

She scooted out her door, hurrying down the hall before any of the other Langston girls could catch sight of her. Then she trotted down the old wooden stairs and out the front door.

It was raining steadily. The air was cold and

heavy and the green was getting muddier. By the time KC reached the dining commons, her tennis shoes were soaked. Then, just as she passed the commons, which was closed up and dark, she remembered that Lauren was working at the Springfield Mountain Inn again that night and wouldn't be in Coleridge Hall anyway.

"Great," KC muttered. "This is a wasted trip."

KC stood on the walkway, letting the rain pour down on her, unsure of where to go next. She'd been working alone in her room all day, not getting much accomplished except a lot of worrying and getting stuck in her own thoughts. She wanted company, but Faith was at rehearsal. KC thought of visiting Faith's neighbor, Kimberly, but Kimberly was in *Alice in Wonderland,* so she'd be at rehearsal, too. No matter how friendly Courtney had been, KC wasn't a Tri Beta yet, and there was no way she could appear on Sorority Row with wet hair and a red, runny nose. And KC would rather have gone back to her single room than go to Forest Hall to drop in on Winnie.

That left the dorm snack bar, a large, overly bright room under the dining commons that was open until midnight. Nobody important ever hung out there, so KC wouldn't have to worry about being seen. It contained snack machines and a counter that sold cold sandwiches, baked goods, candy bars, and drinks.

KC walked down the stairs and went in.

The snack bar was as bright as ever, with banks of fluorescent lights glaring down on beige formica tables and a linoleum floor. A TV flickered over the counter. It was tuned to an old movie, but the sound was turned off. KC bought herself a hot chocolate and a brownie, then looked around for a place to sit.

"That looks like a healthy dinner."

KC looked around.

"Over here."

She finally located Peter Dvorsky, who was sitting by himself at a large, round table. He was holding a magnifying lens up to a contact sheet of black-and-white photos. He wore a big, sloppy turtleneck sweater over a pair of old jeans and an Oakland A's baseball cap.

"Hi," KC answered blandly.

Peter put his lens and his sheet down and stretched.

For no reason KC could figure out, she walked over.

"Sit down," he invited casually.

She hesitated.

"I don't bite."

"But you do hassle."

He held up his hands. "No hassling. Tonight will be hassle-free. I promise."

She set down her cocoa and her brownie.

"I thought girls like you ate only cottage cheese and lettuce leaves."

"Peter."

"Sorry." He smiled. "Sometimes I can't help it. I have hassling in my blood."

KC frowned. "It's okay. I grew up on sprouts and tofu. So now I get cravings for potato chips and chocolate doughnuts. Especially on nights like this."

"Glad to hear it," Peter answered. "I was afraid you were the type who never gave in to something as interesting as a craving."

"Gee, thanks." KC was never sure how to take Peter. But she decided that she didn't mind running into him. He did qualify as company and she didn't have to worry about how awful she looked. She sipped her cocoa. "What's up?"

"Not much." Peter laced his fingers behind his head and yawned. "I skipped dinner to finish a paper for my anthropology class. I came in here to get a sandwich. What are you doing here?"

"I just got restless, I guess," KC admitted. "I've been working on a paper all day, too."

Peter nodded and picked up his contact sheets again.

KC unwrapped her brownie. Something about Peter had really irked her the day he dropped off the calendars. But now that she saw him again she remembered that he was just ordinary Peter, no one to get excited about. And yet, there was still that unimpressed, humorous quality about him that got to her.

"I worked on that paper for six and a half hours," she went on. "I don't think I got anywhere and it's due in a few days. Does that ever happen to you, where you just work and work on something, but it doesn't seem to be happening?"

Peter smiled, but kept right on looking at his pictures. "All the time." He passed one of his contact sheets to her. "The only remedy I know is to keep working."

KC squinted at tiny shots of a snow-capped mountain. Every photo was almost the same, except for tiny variations in angle and light. "These are good."

"No, they're not," Peter explained. He leaned

toward KC to point out details on the photos. His shoulder pressed against hers.

KC didn't move away.

"I took three rolls of Wimer Mountain and I don't have one shot I really like." Peter thought for a moment. "I'm going to hike back up there tomorrow to shoot some more."

KC had to admire Peter's dedication and tenacity. Then, quite suddenly, KC drew in a breath and sneezed. It was a huge, wet sneeze that felt as if it could have taken her head off.

Peter inched back and stared at her.

"Sorry about that!"

He pretended to wring out his shirt, then handed her a stack of napkins. "Talk about hassling."

"I didn't do it on purpose, Peter."

"All right." Peter took back all the napkins except one. "I'm just teasing, KC." He leaned over again and nudged her. "Ever hear of teasing? Sense of humor? As in, don't take everything so seriously?"

KC grabbed the napkin and blew her nose. "Yes, I've heard of it. I think I'm coming down with something."

"I guess that means I'll be coming down with something, too."

"Sorry," KC moaned. "I guess I shouldn't have let my hair get so wet."

"You do look like you just went swimming."

"I stood in the rain," she explained. "Is that unserious enough for you? As in unexplainable, spacey, and dumb?"

"You? Never." Peter sat back and watched her for a long time. "Any particular reason?" he finally asked. "For standing in the rain, I mean."

KC didn't answer right away. "I don't think so." She touched her stringy, wet hair. "How do I know?"

"Well, if you don't know, KC, who does?"

KC looked at him. For the first time she saw something deep and interesting in his eyes. Suddenly, she felt embarrassed. "I look awful, don't I?"

Peter rested his chin in his hands and stared back at her, the same way he'd surveyed her face when he'd taken her picture. "Not really."

"Honest?"

"You know," Peter said, his face taking on a curious smile, "I like you better like this than when you were all made up for that photo."

KC began to feel a little funny. The conversation had taken an odd turn. She wasn't sure where they were headed. "Yeah, sure," she scoffed. Then she crumbled a piece off her brownie and munched on it. "I don't know. Maybe I didn't look so great in that calendar after all. I keep hearing that I have this great chance to be freshman princess at Winter Formal, but it's in less than a week now, and I don't even have a date."

"Do you think that's that the only reason someone would ask you to Winter Formal?" Peter took his contact sheet back and slid it into an envelope. "Because you look great?"

"I don't know."

"Believe it or not, KC, there are more important things than how people look."

KC wasn't sure how to respond. "I just mean, I won't even have a chance at freshman princess if I'm not at the formal. They'll crown someone else."

"If it's such a big deal, I'll go with you," Peter said offhandedly as he stuck his contact sheets back in his bag.

"Right," KC laughed, sure that he was joking. "Don't do me any favors."

"I'm serious," he insisted. "If you're that worried about it, and you have so little time, I'll be your date."

"That's all right," KC sighed. "I'm not desperate. I'll find someone."

Peter suddenly put his hand on her arm. KC was surprised to find that her pulse picked up. She wasn't sure what to say.

"If you think going with me would be a sign of desperation, then forget it," Peter said. "But if you really want to go, let's go. It might be fun."

KC stared at Peter. He was still no Warren Manning, but he definitely had his own appeal. And she'd had a better time with him over the last few minutes than she'd had with anyone else lately. He wasn't her idea of a glamorous date, but he was easygoing, talented, and interesting. In a pinch, he was certainly better than nothing.

"Okay," KC decided. "Sure. Why not? Let's go."

"Let's go."

"That's what I said, Peter."

"Let's go."

"Yes. Let's go."

"Is there an echo in here?"

"Peter."

# Seven

*ough, sniff, cough.*

Melissa still wasn't over her cold. From one end of her dorm room to the other, it looked like a medical ward. Vitamins, flowers, tissues, cough drops, herbal teas, even a humidifier that hissed—all of it had been provided by Brooks.

"Mel, what are you doing?" Brooks asked. He was sitting at Winnie's desk doing some drafting homework for his architecture class while Melissa read her chem assignment.

Melissa put her chemistry book away. She got up and began rummaging through her closet.

While Brooks stared, she kicked off her slippers and reached for her training shoes and her track parka. "I think I'm going to the gym."

"No, you're not," he responded easily. He tossed back his blond curls, smiled, and went back to his drafting, as if the subject were closed.

Melissa dropped her shoes and collapsed back on the end of her bed. "What do you mean, no, I'm not?"

Brooks smiled. "I mean, you're not well enough yet. You had a temperature yesterday. You're not ready to go to the gym yet. Besides, it's too late to walk across campus. It's dark out."

"I always go to the gym at night, Brooks. And I didn't have a temperature today."

He shrugged. "Mel, you're still sick. Wait a few more days."

"A few more days! In a few more days I'll have lost a few more seconds from my race time." Melissa took a deep breath. "Brooks, I'm not going to sprint naked through the rain. I'm not going to run a marathon in the pitch dark. I just want to do an easy weight workout before my muscles start shriveling up." Despite herself, she began to cough.

"See what I mean?" Brooks said. He closed his book and climbed onto the bed behind her. He began to massage her back gently. "How's that?" he whispered.

"Nice. It's all nice. The flowers are nice. The soup was nice. The juice and the tea and the vitamins are nice. But it's possible to have too much nice, Brooks. I just want to go over to the smelly, un-nice gym and lift some weights." Melissa jerked away from him, tugged on her shoes, and started for the door.

Brooks stopped her with a more serious tone. "Melissa, this isn't a joke. You're still sick. You can't go and work out yet. You shouldn't even be out of bed."

She spun back to face him. "Who are you to tell me what I can and can't do, Brooks?"

His face tensed in anger. "I'm not trying to tell you what to do!"

"Oh really? You just said I couldn't go work out yet. That sounds like an order to me. And you have no right to order me around."

Brooks stood up. "I'm not ordering you around, Mel. I'm concerned about you. Why do you think I keep bringing you vitamins and tea and everything? Because I care. I just want you to get better."

"Well, Brooks," Melissa snapped. "I want to get better, too."

Before Brooks could stop her, Melissa grabbed her gym bag and walked out.

"This is good punch."
"It even has little berries in it."
"What kind are they?"
"Berry berries."
"Excuse me?"
"Yogi Berries."
"Oh."
"How about term-paper *cram*- berries?"
"You must be a writer."
"A journalist."
"Of course. After all, this is the campus-newspaper party."
"Ten points for you."
"Do you write under a byline?"
Dash held up his cup. "No. Under a party *punch* line."
"What?"
"Never mind." Dash Ramirez laughed alone at his own joke. The girl he was talking to over a slice of burnt pizza was pretty. Her name was Susan Cohn. She wore big hoop earrings and had a radical sixties look. She had on wide green army pants and a print blouse that looked antique. Her hair was short on top and long on the

sides—kind of like an Afghan hound. But Susan was no dog. She was attractive and bright and a neighbor of Alison Argonbright and Richard Levine, the two radical reporters who were hosting the *U of S Weekly Journal* party.

"So you're a friend of Alison and Richard?" Dash asked, forcing himself to make conversation.

Susan nodded, her mouth remaining in a straight horizontal line. "I live upstairs. I plan to join the Progressive Students' Coalition. I want to get involved in causes."

"*Any* progressive cause?"

Susan didn't pick up on his sarcasm. She sipped her cranberry punch and kept on talking. "I can't believe the number of people on this campus who are apathetic about politics and the outside world. As long as their little football games and dances and grades are okay, the rest of the world can just rot."

Dash shrugged. "And we newspaper people are so serious."

Susan pushed ahead with her serious theme. "Alison and Richard told me that you've been involved with the coalition, too," she said. "They said that you were in a demonstration that kept some old people in the neighborhood from losing their homes. They said the university wanted to move them just so they could build another parking lot."

"Yeah." Dash was barely listening, even though he should have been making the moves on her, and had intended to make the moves on her when she'd approached him. He was clean-shaven for once, and dressed in something besides an ink-stained T-shirt. The only reason he'd come to this party was to get his mind off Lauren by looking around for somebody else. He told himself to ignore the fact that Susan was humorless and boring and just go for it. Otherwise he was going to mope around uselessly for the rest of the semester.

"So what do you do on the newspaper?" Susan asked when she realized that his attention was waning.

"I'm an assistant editor."

"I see."

"And sometimes I write."

"What do you write about?"

"Whatever the paper wants me to write about." Dash sighed.

Susan raised her voice, since the entertainment editor had begun singing along with the party tape. "Alison and Richard told me that you just published a story about a terrible hazing incident on Fraternity Row. That must have been very exciting to investigate."

Dash couldn't take it anymore. Lauren had done all the investigating for the article. Brave, sensitive, shy, smart, mysterious, two-timing Lauren.

"Yeah, well," Dash answered, clapping his hands together, "nice talking to you. I think I'll go outside and get some air."

"But it's raining outside."

"Is it? That's okay. I like the rain."

Susan looked hurt. She had one of those was-it-my-breath? kind of expressions on her face. Dash felt like putting his hand on her shoulder and saying, *It's nothing personal. I'm just so weirded out over what happened with Lauren. You'd be weirded out, too, if the person you were crazy about had lied about who she was and then betrayed you with another guy. A fraternity guy, no less.* But he didn't say a word. Instead, he turned around and wandered away.

Dash walked across the living room, which wasn't a very long walk, since Alison and Richard's apartment was small, with a low ceiling and dark wood paneling on the walls. It seemed like a place where hotshot reporters and radicals would hang out, where plots would be hatched, conspiracies agreed upon, and manifestos written.

But that Sunday night it was full of revelers laughing and talking about all the things that every other college student talked about: papers, skiing, grades, dates for Winter Formal.

" 'Scuse, please," Dash mumbled, shouldering his way through the crowd.

The problem with girls like Susan was that they assumed that if you were involved in politics or the newspaper, that was all you cared about. But Dash also liked football and music. He liked ethnic food, funny movies, weird ties, motorcycles, history, and pulp detective novels.

Dash had sensed that Lauren would like all those things, too, or at least some of them. When he'd first met Lauren, he'd known that she had writing talent. Even though she was rich, he'd also sensed that she had moral conviction and heart. She seemed so innocent and fresh, yet ready for whatever might come her way. Of course, Dash hadn't predicted then that her innocence might have been just an act. He hadn't expected her to turn out to be a fake.

Dash made it to the front door and went outside. It wasn't really raining any longer. There was just a fine mist that hung in the air and puddles that had settled in front of the porch. Dash looked up at the dark sky, then blew on his cold hands.

"Oh man."

Dash had always thought of himself as hardheaded, savvy, and streetwise, so he still couldn't believe that Lauren had faked him out. She'd pretended to have given up her pampered upbringing and her sorority, when in all probability she hadn't changed at all. At least that's what Dash assumed. Still, there was no doubt about one thing. Lauren had seemed to be wild about him, and in the end he'd caught her red-handed. With his own eyes, he'd seen her kissing Christopher Hammond.

"Christopher Hammond," Dash muttered. He sat down on the damp wooden stoop. "Of all the big jerks on campus, he's one of the jerkiest." Christopher, the big-deal Interfraternity Council officer, was handsome, popular, and as shallow as the puddle by Dash's foot. Christopher was also irresistible to just about every girl on campus, and now that list included Lauren. It made Dash sick to think about it.

"Maybe I should just go home," he concluded.

Slowly, Dash began to stand, then crouched down again as he saw someone turn off the sidewalk and head for Alison and Richard's apartment house. For a moment Dash thought it was Lauren, even though he told himself that Lauren was just on his mind so much lately that he thought he saw her everywhere he looked. Dash huffed and put his chin in his hands. He didn't want to think about Lauren anymore.

The girl coming up the steps was wearing an expensive raincoat with the collar turned up. She carried a small leather shoulder bag and a big brown paper sack. She trotted right by Dash without looking at him and put her hand out for the doorknob.

Then she turned back.

Dash froze.

"Dash?"

It *was* Lauren. Dash sat up, but didn't speak. For a long time neither of them said anything. There was just the muffled noise of the party inside the house and the sound of the breeze ruffling some wet leaves.

Finally Dash heard the rustle of paper and a couple of footsteps. Lauren walked back down to the bottom step and faced him. She clutched her paper sack as if she were a toddler hugging a stuffed animal.

"Hey," he said.

"Dash."

Dash couldn't help raising his head and staring at Lauren's fine, pale skin. Her fluffy hair had gone haywire from the humidity, and even in the dim porch light he could see the exquisite violet color of her eyes. She wasn't wearing her glasses, and under her open coat he could see that she had on baggy dark pants and an oversized sweater. Something red and lace-trimmed stuck out of the top of the paper sack. Dash was confused again by her half-sorority girl, half-campus radical appearance.

"Am I early?" she said in her whispery, refined voice.

"I don't think so. The party's in full swing. Swing on in."

Lauren didn't move. "I have to go to work tonight, so I had to come early. I can't stay long."

"You have a job?"

"A part-time job."

"Good for you."

She shifted. "Not really. Um, I'm working at the Springfield Mountain Inn Friday, Saturday, and Sunday nights . . . as a chambermaid." She gestured to the clothes in the paper sack. "This is the uniform they make me wear. It's pretty dumb."

"I thought maybe it was your disguise," Dash taunted, "so you could leave here, change, and go straight over to the Tri Betas."

A flash of pain ran across Lauren's face. Their eyes met briefly and then both of them looked away again. Dash felt like crawling under the porch. Surely Lauren would walk away now. He almost wished she would. Then at least it would be over.

Instead, Lauren leaned against the railing and looked out into the street.

Dash waited while a car drove by, sending a muddy spray within a few feet of them.

"I'm not going over to the sorority," Lauren finally said sadly. "For your information, I quit the sorority, just like I said I would. And my mother cut off all my money, just like she said she would."

"What?" Dash's head popped up. Lauren had never told him anything about her mother threatening to cut her off financially.

Lauren looked right at him. "I'm on my own now. I'm not getting any help from my parents at all. I sold my car, or what was left of my car after my friend Winnie crashed it, and now I have this job. I just hope I can make enough money to make it through the end of my freshman year."

"You mean your parents only wanted to support you if you stayed in the sorority? But I thought they were so rich."

Lauren shrugged. "It's because they're so rich that they figure they can control me with money." She bit her lip and tears filled her eyes. "But that's not important. What is important is that I wanted to apologize for kissing that creep Christopher Hammond. I know you think I'm some kind of phony, but I barely know Christopher Hammond. He was just trying to get me to stop doing the hazing article and I didn't know how to stop him. It was my own fault. I don't even like him."

Dash's head began to reel. He wasn't sure what to believe anymore, or what to do. He reached out, almost touching Lauren's arm. Then he drew his hand back.

Lauren blushed. Dash had seen her redden like that before. He felt a pang in his heart.

They were both silent again, then Lauren moved away from the rail. "I guess I should go in. I don't have much time and I wanted to say hello to Alison and Richard."

Dash nodded. He wanted to stop her, to have

her sit down again and explain everything to him. He wanted her by his side, to talk to and reason with, to share his ideas, his feelings, and his jokes. But at the same time he wanted to be tough. He wanted to be Dash the hardheaded reporter. He wanted to be impenetrable Dash Ramirez, even though he felt like Dash the avocado-head.

Lauren hesitated on the top step. "It's good to see you," she said.

"You, too."

"Well, goodnight," Lauren added, even though she continued to stand by the door.

"Go on in," Dash said as he got up to leave. "There's berry punch in there."

"That sounds berry nice," Lauren came back.

Dash watched her open the door and go inside. In spite of himself, he stared after her for the longest time and smiled.

# Eight

"Uh-oh," Winnie whispered, slumping down in her seat. The mood in the Western Civ lecture hall had grown tense. The teaching assistant was walking down the aisles, her arms full of corrected blue books.

"Here we go," Faith sighed.

"I think I did okay on this one," peeped Lauren. "But Hermann gives so many exams, you never know for sure."

KC blew her nose, then stared straight ahead.

"Our exams are coming back to haunt us." Winnie continued to chatter nervously. The TA was getting closer.

"Maybe we should all go to the student union afterward and bury our cares in a huge order of nachos." Winnie grinned. "Whoever gets the best grade has to pay."

"Winnie, shhh!"

"KC, don't shush me. We're getting back exams, not watching brain surgery. I can talk."

"That's an understatement," KC grumbled. She rubbed her bleary eyes, trying not to smudge her makeup.

Winnie threw back her head and her Fred and Barney earrings swung from side to side. "Give me a break, KC. What's the problem? Will it violate some secret sorority rule if one of us sees your grade?"

"I don't care who sees my grade," KC insisted.

"You just care if I see it, right?" Winnie scowled. "I realize that I'm a dishonest, untrustworthy person because I talk too much, I stay out too late, I still haven't told Josh the truth about Travis, and whatever other sins you suddenly think I'm guilty of. But if you want so much privacy, why don't you just sit by yourself? I don't want your cold anyway."

The TA had almost reached their row. Lauren and Faith were looking back and forth between the blue books and KC and Winnie's argument.

KC leaned forward. She blew her nose. "If I'd wanted privacy, Winnie, I wouldn't be hanging out with you."

"I was beginning to wonder if you still *were* hanging out with me," Winnie shot back.

The spat ended abruptly, because the TA was at the end of their row calling out names. Faith sprang to her feet and sidled over to retrieve her blue book. Lauren waited for hers to be passed along. Winnie lunged, reaching over four other students to grab hers, while KC sat as still as a block of ice, finally taking her blue book from the TA and barely glancing inside.

"Well?" Winnie questioned when the TA had gone on to the next row.

Lauren slowly opened hers. Then she let her head fall back in exaggerated relief. "I got an A minus."

Faith applauded and Winnie pumped a victorious fist.

Faith peeked at her grade, then gave a good-natured shrug. "I got a B."

"There's nothing wrong with that." Winnie glanced briefly at KC. Then she folded back the first page of her exam and gasped. She held the pages up against her chest. There, for all to see, was a big, fat A.

"Winnie, congratulations." Faith grinned.

Lauren patted Winnie and laughed.

KC still sat staring straight ahead as Dr. Hermann began writing an outline on the board.

"KC, how did you do?" Faith finally asked.

KC slipped her blue book in her briefcase and took out some blank paper. Her gray eyes looked hard and steely. "Not as well as I'd hoped," she stated. "I only got a B plus."

---

"B plus," KC muttered a few hours later as she wandered alongside the pioneer graveyard on her way back to the dorms. Her nose was even runnier and her head was beginning to feel as if it had been stuffed with hay. "I only wish I'd gotten a B plus. Or just a plain old B. Even a B minus wouldn't have been so bad."

She kicked a clod of mud and kept on walking. At least the rain had stopped, even though the sky was still overcast and the ground was soaked. KC felt bogged down, too. In reality she'd gotten a C on her exam for Western Civ. A C wasn't good enough for graduate business school. It wasn't good enough for the Tri Betas. And it certainly wasn't good enough for KC Angeletti.

As KC passed the new computer center and turned onto the dorm green, she did some quick math in her head to figure out her grade-point average. This first semester would end soon. Who knew how finals would go, but so far, the only class she was doing well in was Introduction to Business. At least she was heading for an A there. But she'd only gotten a C plus on her English lit midterm, and she had the feeling that the results of her accounting exam might be a lot worse than that.

"I don't know how I'll ever bring my average up." She swung her briefcase and walked faster. "I'll just have to try harder when it comes to finals."

KC stopped when the three complexes of dorms came into view. She stared at the brick fifties-style dorms, where Coleridge Hall stood out with its arty banners and brightly colored wall murals. Beyond that were the sterile new dorms, such as Forest Hall, where Winnie and Melissa lived. Closest were the quaint old dorms, such as KC's, Langston House. The old dorms had originally been administration buildings when the university had first opened. They were charming houses with wooden porches and high, peaked roofs.

KC had almost reached her dorm when she decided to head over to Coleridge Hall instead.

She wanted to talk to someone—she needed to talk to someone.

As she continued to walk, however, she realized she wasn't heading over to talk to Faith or Lauren or Kimberly.

She was on her way to talk to Peter Dvorsky.

*Well, there's nothing wrong with that,* KC thought. *I'm going to Winter Formal with him. Why shouldn't he and I have another conversation?*

KC sidestepped a mudhole. She stomped on some wet grass and stopped worrying about getting muddy. Peter might not be impressed by her looks and sudden campus fame, but even though that was mildly annoying, it also meant that he didn't expect her to look perfect or not have a runny nose or get straight As. And that made KC feel a lot more free. Even with Faith and Winnie she felt obligated to keep up a front. With Peter, KC might be able to talk about a few of the problems that were really on her mind.

But when KC passed the sturdy wooden stairs that led up to the porch of Langston House, she saw something that was on her mind just as much as grades, Courtney and the Tri Betas, Peter, or Winnie.

It was Warren Manning.

KC's heart rocked. Warren looked so handsome sitting on the porch railing with his arms folded over his heavy sweater and sport coat, his dark hair perfectly combed, that KC could have stared at him forever.

Still, she didn't stare. She blinked and headed over to Langston House, but didn't dare slow down. What if Warren's being there, posing on the porch like a model ready for a GQ cover shoot, had nothing to do with her? What if he were waiting for someone else?

KC kept walking. After all, she lived in Langston House. If Warren wasn't there to see her, she could scoot past him without embarrassment and hurry on up to her room.

"There you are, KC," Warren cried when she got closer. He leapt off the railing and smiled.

KC felt something that was halfway between fabulous excitement and relief. She held her feelings in check, though, and managed a mere cool smile as she sauntered up to join him. She prayed that she wouldn't sneeze or be forced to wipe her nose with her sleeve.

"Here I am," she said, offering Warren a polite handshake. She practically held her breath.

"Here you are," Warren repeated. He held on to her hand long after the shake was over, looking her up and down in appreciation. "You wouldn't believe what I had to go through to find you."

"Wouldn't I?"

He kissed the top of her hand, looking down at her with sleepy eyes.

KC smiled.

Then Warren leaned on the porch railing and stuck his hands in the pockets of his wool slacks. Every move he made was so classy and graceful that it seemed choreographed. "I tried to call you, but your dorm phone is always busy."

"Is it?"

"I called you twice. Twice!" Warren shook his head. "I almost never call girls twice if I can't get through. And I certainly don't call a third time."

"I'm honored." KC decided to strike a pose of her own. She set down her briefcase and considered propping her foot on it. Then she looked down and saw that her ankle was splattered with mud, so she set her briefcase in front of her feet instead. She knew that despite her red nose the rest of her looked good.

"This was my last resort," Warren said, looking off at the green. "If I didn't find you here, I was going to give up."

"Give up on what?" KC tossed back.

Warren gave her a sly smile. He pulled a rolled-up magazine from the pocket of his sport coat and opened it to a fashion photograph of a man standing by a fountain, holding the hand of a stunning young woman in a simple silver gown. "That could be us."

"Oh really?" KC leaned in, her dark hair brushing against Warren's lapel. She read the caption. "It says they're standing in front of some fountain in Milan, Italy. Are you inviting me on a trip to Milan?"

He laughed. "Maybe someday I will. I'll probably work in Milan."

"Doing what?"

"Modeling."

"Really?" KC smothered a fierce sneeze. Warren was still studying the magazine. "Is that what you want to do? Do you want to be a professional model?"

He nodded, barely looking up. "I'd be doing it right now if my parents weren't forcing me to get my degree in advertising first. They keep saying I need to work for a living. I say to them, being a model is hard work. You have to make contacts. You have to keep everything about your body in perfect shape. You need the right clothes for the interview, the right photos for your portfolio. It's not like you just show up and stand there."

KC had modeled for a department store in high school, but she'd only seen it as a way to make extra cash. "How interesting."

"Yeah." Warren pushed up his sleeve to check his watch. "Anyway, I didn't come over here to talk about modeling."

"Oh? What does bring you all the way to my dorm?"

Warren faced her and smiled. "I came over to ask you to Winter Formal."

KC's pulse went wild. She tried to maintain her cool composure, but her insides had gone crazy. "What?"

"I know it's late," Warren said, "and that I should have asked you way before this. But I only saw you last week, and like I said, I tried to call twice. Obviously a gorgeous girl like you already has a date—"

"Actually, I do," KC blurted as she simultaneously wondered how she could get out of it.

Warren looked right at her. "Break it."

KC felt a lurch in her stomach when she thought about Peter. She tried to tell herself that Peter had asked her only to help her out of a fix. There was nothing between them, and Peter would probably be relieved to be let off the hook.

Still, she couldn't quite convince herself that she should break the date with him.

Warren showed her the magazine again. "Do you want to simply show up at Winter Formal, or do you want to *appear*, looking like this?"

"I . . ." KC stared at the photo, trying to find something that would tell her that it was all right to cancel her date with Peter.

Warren took her hand. "I know you have a chance at freshman princess. If you show up with me, there's no way you'll be overlooked."

KC looked up at Warren and felt more confused than ever.

"I'm wearing a black cutaway," Warren whispered. "With a red tie. We can figure out matching scarves or something like that at the last minute. I can get a girl who works at Fredericka's downtown to make them for us. She's wild about me. She'll do me a favor anytime."

"But I haven't said I'd go with you yet," KC stammered, sniffling in spite of herself.

"Yes, you have." Warren leaned in and kissed her. Then he touched her chin and looked at her with his dazzling, photogenic face. "You said yes the first time you laid eyes on me."

KC knew that he was right.

# Nine

ow dare she!”

“Marielle, can you just look at skis and forget about stupid Courtney Conner for five minutes?”

“No, I can’t, Mark. Can you just forget about your stupid skis for five minutes and talk to me about Courtney Conner?”

“Geez, Marielle.”

“Mark!”

“All right, all right.” Mark Geisslinger pulled on his mustache, then turned to the salesman in the downtown Springfield Ski Hut. “Look, man, hold onto that pair of skis for me, will you? I'll be back later."

The salesman nodded and carted the skis into the back.

Marielle stormed away, past the parkas and the boots, the sweaters and the poles. She went straight out the front door and took off, hurrying down the sidewalk.

"Marielle, wait up," Mark called.

Marielle strode faster.

*"Marielle!"* Mark began to run.

So did Marielle. In her high heels and short, straight skirt, it wasn't easy. Her legs strained against her hem as she ran past a new-car lot, a fast-food restaurant, and a Dino's Chicken stand.

Mark quickly caught up to her and grabbed her arms. "What is your problem?"

"I told you what my problem was, but you weren't interested." She pouted and pushed him away. Then she decided to change her tactics. She imitated Mark's body language, slumping with one hand in a pretend pocket and a surly scowl on her face. She flirted with her eyes.

"Marielle," Mark said, starting to crack a smile.

Marielle imitated his macho walk and moved closer. At the last moment she dropped her anger and threw her arms around him. She kissed his neck, then pretended to bite him.

Mark tried to back away, but ended up grabbing her and kissing her right in front of a store window. Two older women looking at furniture stopped to stare. "You drive me crazy, you crazy woman," Mark admitted.

Marielle pushed him away and laughed. "I know. And that's why you're going to listen to me about how much I hate Courtney Conner and how she is a total pain in the rear. She's a perfect little dictatorial snob who is trying to ruin my life and ruin my sorority. In that order."

"Yeah, yeah, yeah."

Marielle grabbed his cable-knit sweater with two fists. "I'm serious, Mark. Courtney thinks that just because she's president of the Tri Betas she can tell me what I can do, who I can like, what's right and wrong, who should pledge our house." Marielle threw her head back and screamed. "I can't believe I ever voted for her. Courtney wouldn't know a decent pledge if the girl came up and punched her in the nose."

Mark took Marielle's hand and moved down the block to sit on a bus-stop bench.

Marielle went with him, talking the whole way. "I tried to save the house by getting rid of that pathetic Lauren Turnbell-Smythe, and do I get thanks for it?"

Mark shrugged.

"No," Marielle answered, plopping down next to him. "I got nothing but a snotty little lecture and the most humiliating snub in front of KC Angeletti. KC Angeletti! Ugh, that burns me up. It makes me sick." She slid closer to Mark and put her hand on his knee. "Lauren is the reason you got caught hazing and have to do twenty hours of stupid community service. You think about Lauren Turnbell-Smythe and how much Courtney loves her when you're emptying bed-pans at the hospital and serving watery spaghetti to the homeless."

Mark cringed.

"Right." Marielle leaned forward. "Courtney now thinks that Lauren is Joan of Arc or something. And Courtney acts like I'm Jack the Ripper just because I tried to keep that traitor out of our house."

Mark nodded.

"But do you know who else Courtney thinks is just great now?"

"Who?"

"The freshman lowlife I just mentioned. Lauren's friend. That phony Kahia Cayanne Angeletti."

"Who?"

"KC Angeletti!" Marielle slid closer and lowered her twangy voice. "The girl who dropped that tray of drinks on us during fall rush."

"Oh yeah. That's one woman who pushed me too far."

"I know. And I just bet KC helped Lauren Turnbell-Smythe get that hazing story," Marielle insisted. "That's the gossip, anyway, and as far as I've ever known, gossip almost always turns out to be true."

Mark looked at her.

Marielle took his hand. "I do know for sure that KC was the one who snitched to Faith Crowley about seeing Christopher flirt with some girl at the same party where you guys hazed Howard Benmann. It was right after that that Faith Crowley dumped Christopher. And did you know that snitchy KC and Faith are friends who grew up in the same dingy little town?"

"Oh yeah?" Mark's dark eyes widened with interest. Christopher Hammond was his roommate at the ODT fraternity. "Christopher's not used to getting dumped. He wasn't very happy about it."

Marielle grinned. "Just my point! And now Courtney is acting as if she and KC are best friends or something. Courtney wants KC in the Tri Betas so badly she'd give up her Lady Clairol for it."

Mark laughed.

"This isn't funny," Marielle stressed, beginning to laugh, too. "Think about it, Mark. KC Angeletti hurt Christopher. She turned Courtney against me. She insulted you and me during fall rush and then she helped Lauren get you in trouble. And now what do you think KC is going to get in return?"

"Trouble, I hope."

"No! She's going to get invited into the Tri Betas after spring rush. She's going to be one of the most sought-after freshmen on campus because of her dumb calendar. And she's going to win freshman princess at the Winter Formal. What do you think of that?"

Mark squinted at the cars and thought.

*"Mark."*

"It sucks," he finally announced.

"You're telling me," Marielle agreed. "Which is why we have to do something about it. And we have to do something soon. Winter Formal is this Friday night. We don't have much time."

Mark put his arm around her. "We don't, do we."

Marielle smiled.

Mark's mustache turned up as he broke into a nasty grin.

That night the light in the Beanery was grainy with cigarette smoke. The smell of dark ground coffee was overpowering, while the sound of Travis Bennett's singing voice was sensual, raspy, and low.

Winnie was sitting alone at a corner table. She'd left her dorm on impulse, tiptoeing past Josh's door, but then running into Mikoto in the lobby. She'd told Mikoto that she was heading out to get cough medicine for Melissa. As soon as she was outside, she'd sprinted over the dorm green and then jogged all the way across campus to the Beanery. When she'd arrived, her back was damp from drizzle and sweat. Her feet hurt from running in her soft-soled boots. Her short hair was even spikier than usual and her long earrings were tangled up.

Nonetheless, Winnie felt calm. She'd gathered her nerve. She knew she loved Josh. KC could no longer accuse her of being a liar or a fake. Waiting, she sipped herb tea, listened to a new song that Travis had written, and played with the candle wax.

"Goodbye, Travis Bennett," she mouthed silently as she watched him.

Travis's long hair looked beautiful in the spotlight as he leaned over his acoustic guitar to play a riff between the verses. He'd been so concentrated on his performance that he hadn't seen her come in. Winnie liked being able to watch him from a distance. It helped prepare her for what she was about to do.

Travis's song came to end. After the enthusiastic applause, he put his guitar down and leaned into the microphone. "Thanks, folks. That song was inspired by a girl I met in Paris last summer. She goes to school here in Springfield and she's pretty special." He paused. "Order lots of coffee and I'll see you in twenty minutes for another set."

Lighter applause followed as he stepped off the tiny stage and headed toward the kitchen. Halfway there he turned and stopped, staring right at Winnie as if he'd suddenly become aware of her through the back of his head. He stood staring while a waiter walked by and some students bunched around a big table laughed. Travis stuck his hands in the pockets of his baggy black pants and walked over to Winnie.

"Hi, beautiful. Anybody sitting here?" he asked, referring to the other chair at Winnie's table.

Winnie shook her head.

He slowly sat down. "I wondered if I'd ever see you again. I've been waiting for you to come by. I didn't want to bug you if you didn't want me in your life."

"It's not that," Winnie said evasively.

He leaned forward. "Then what is it? I haven't seen you since you got back from break. My gig here ends next Monday. I need to know what's going on, Win."

Winnie didn't answer.

He reached for her hand. "Look at me, beautiful. Talk to me. Don't jerk me around."

*I'm a chicken,* Winnie thought as she finally looked up and took in the romantic intensity of Travis's blue eyes. Last summer Winnie would have followed Travis anywhere, gladly sharing the thrilling highs and the desperate lows. Now, however, the mellow in-betweens were beginning to look much more appealing to her.

"I don't want to jerk you around, Travis."

"Then just tell me how you feel, Win. That's what counts with me."

Winnie sipped her tea and was silent.

Travis sighed. "Is there somebody else?"

Winnie still was unable to speak. In high school she'd been dumped and lied to so many times that she couldn't totally let go of a great guy who was still in love with her, even though she was in love with someone else.

"It doesn't have anything to do with me, or someone else, or how I feel," she lied. "It has to do with your career. You need to go to Los Angeles to try and make it in the music business, and you need to go now. That's more important than you or me or how we feel."

"Is that really what you think, Win?"

Winnie began to cry. "Promise me you'll go, Travis. Soon. As soon as your gig here is finished. Will you do that for me? You're too good a musician to waste your time in little coffeehouses like this. You should be making records and playing big clubs." She caught her breath and looked at him again. "Do you believe me? Will you go?"

"You want me to go just because of my career?" Travis questioned. "That's the only reason?"

Winnie hesitated. "Well . . . yes."

# Ten

Everywhere KC looked she saw something that reminded her of Winter Formal. Posters announcing the big do had gone up all over campus. There were formal-dress displays in downtown store windows. There was even a photographic layout from past Winter Formals on the walls of the Springfield Print Shop, where KC had gone to meet Matthew Kallender, the creator of the U of S Classic Calendar.

"So Winter Formal is coming up," Matthew mentioned. He and KC were standing at the print-shop counter, picking up another order of calendars. Matthew was twisting his blond rat-tail between his fingers and humming some corny old song that he thought was "classic."

"What?"

"Winter Formal."

"Sorry, Matthew," KC apologized. "I'm so stuffed up that I can't hear very well. I've got that stupid cold that's going around campus. I'd better be over it by Friday."

"I was talking about you and Peter Dvorsky," Matthew repeated. "I heard you're going to Winter Formal together."

"Where did you hear that?"

"Peter told me. He seemed pretty excited about it."

"He did?" KC's stomach dropped. Peter excited? About going out with her? Over and over she'd told herself that Peter wouldn't care if she broke their date. He'd only asked her as a favor. He wasn't impressed by her. He barely even liked her.

And how did she feel about him—about ordinary Peter Dvorsky?

KC had been avoiding Peter ever since she'd accepted Warren's invitation. For some reason she still hadn't told Peter that she was breaking their date and going to Winter Formal with someone else.

The print-shop manager handed a stack of calendars to Matthew, who flipped through the pages, checking the quality. "The talented photographer and his beautiful model," Matthew commented, pausing at KC's photo. "It's classic."

"How about the smart model and her talented photographer?" KC spat back, hoping to change the subject. "Don't be so sexist, Matthew."

Matthew thought for a moment. "Sexism is classic, too."

KC shook her head.

Matthew paid the print-shop man, then kept his wallet open and turned to KC.

"Here's your share so far, Madame Consultant." Matthew began counting out bills. "You get twenty cents per calendar, so that comes to two hundred and twelve dollars."

"Great." KC took the money and breathed a sigh of relief. It would take at least two hundred dollars to outfit her for the formal, especially now that she was going with Warren. And, no matter what, she'd decided that she *was* going with gorgeous Warren. She'd be a fool not to go with him.

"Thank you," said Matthew, doing a corny bow. "Your brilliant input was worth every penny."

KC perked up a little. "I'm glad."

Matthew didn't put his wallet away. "Listen, KC, I've got some appointments today with shops downtown to see if we can pick up a few last-minute sales. I think we've finally saturated the campus. Everybody's too busy now writing papers and thinking about Winter Formal."

*Winter Formal again!*

Matthew folded another stack of bills and stuck it in an envelope. "Anyway, this is Peter's share of the profits so far. I said I'd get it to him today so he can buy some new camera lens or something, but I'm not heading back to the dorms. Can you stop by Peter's dorm and drop it off for me?"

KC's whole body stiffened.

"Of course you can." Matthew put his wallet away and checked his fat appointment book. "Thanks, KC. You're classic."

*Knock, knock, knock.*

A half-hour later KC stood outside Peter's dorm room and held her breath.

"Peter?" she called.

When she didn't get an answer, she cleared her throat and called again. *"Peter."*

Nothing.

KC looked up and down the hall. She hadn't spent much time on the first floor of Coleridge Hall, since Faith and Lauren lived upstairs and the ground floor was guys only. There were pieces of sculpture stacked in a corner and abstract murals on the walls. The smell of paint hung in the air and she could hear someone practicing scales on an oboe.

KC considered sliding the envelope of money under Peter's door and making a quick exit, but she knew she couldn't avoid him much longer. She'd waited too long already to give Peter the news about Winter Formal. If she waited much longer she might as well just stand him up. With every passing hour she felt like even more of a sleaze.

She knocked again, so hard that she hurt her knuckles. Finally, when she was just about to leave, she heard a door open down the hall and saw Peter walk out from what she realized was the dorm darkroom. He was wearing an old football jersey and jeans and drying his hands with a towel.

"KC," Peter said. He walked faster and tossed

the towel over his shoulder. "A visit from Miss March. Or was it Miss April?"

"Peter."

They lingered in the hall.

"The way you're dressed, you look like Miss Chamber of Commerce."

KC shifted in her jacket and dress-for-success tie. "Don't start, okay?" She sneezed.

Peter reached in his pocket and handed her a piece of lens-cleaning tissue. "I'm flattered that you came to visit me. Come into my parlor and sneeze away. How'd you finally do on that Western Civ paper? Did you turn it in?"

"I'm turning it in tomorrow." KC relaxed a little. Peter seemed to be the only person she might be able to talk to about her grade worries. "It's done. Actually I don't know what else to do with it, so I guess it's done."

"Do you want me to read it tonight?" Peter offered. "I'm no history genius, but I took Western Civ last year and I can tell you if I think your paper makes sense or not."

"That's okay."

"If you change your mind, just bring it over." Peter dug for his key. "Hey, you have to talk to me about Friday night. I realized after we decided to go to this thing together that the night is almost upon us, and that I don't know anything about it. What time does this thing start? Am I supposed to rent a tux? I hope we can walk over there because all I have is a motorcycle."

"You ride a motorcycle?"

He nodded. "It drives my parents crazy. But I always wear my helmet. If you want, I'll take you for a ride."

"No thanks," KC had never thought of Peter as the kind of guy who rode a motorcycle. An old Schwinn three-speed maybe, but not a motorcycle.

"Okay. Anyway, I can rent a tux if I have to." Peter finally opened his door and led the way in. "I'd better just call downtown and reserve one before they run out of my size."

KC took a step into Peter's room, then stopped. He lived in a small single room, like she did. But unlike her bare walls, every inch of available space in his room was covered with a photograph. There were photos of Yellowstone Park, of sad and unusual people, of wild horses, of the Mount St. Helens volcano, and of abstract black-and-white shapes of shadow and light. Peter's photographs were moving and beautiful.

There were also contact sheets from the calendar photo sessions. A proof sheet was up for each model with the final picture circled in red. KC's sheet was mixed in with the rest of them, no more important, no less.

Peter cleared some clothes off his bed and sat down. "Sorry this place is a mess. When I'm working on photos, I don't think too much about anything else."

"I see." KC sat on his desk chair, still staring at the photos. "You know, your photos are wonderful."

He looked around. "Some of them are okay. I have a pretty good eye. And if you take enough pictures, you're bound to get something interesting, something important."

KC didn't know what else to say. She sniffled and wiped her nose with her hand. Her head was beginning to feel cloudy and her eyes had begun to water. She opened her briefcase and reached for the envelope Matthew had given her. "Here's your cut of the calendar profits. Matthew asked me to give it to you."

Peter took the envelope and peeked inside. "All right. Not bad. Thanks."

"Sure." KC sat tall, with her hands folded and her eyes downcast. As the oboist stopped his practice session and an opera singer began, KC still sat, feeling every second tick away as if a bomb were about to go off. In spite of herself, she was intrigued by Peter. She admired him. And yet she was still sure that she *had* to go to the formal with Warren. Freshman princess and membership in the Tri Betas depended on appearances. Nonetheless, KC suddenly wished that Winter Formal didn't exist. She cleared her throat.

"So what did you come here to tell me, KC?" Peter finally asked. "You're starting to act fairly weird, in case you think I don't notice. Not that you don't always act somewhat weird, but I can usually brush it off. Right now, though, you're starting to make me feel weird, too."

"That's not my problem," KC came back defensively.

Peter sat forward and stared at her with his perceptive photographer's eyes. "Yes, it is your problem. And I have a feeling it's my problem, too. So, out with it."

KC was unable to speak.

"KC, if you came here to say something, just say it. I don't want to sit here all night staring at you. I know you're nice to look at, but believe me, I have more important things to do."

"All right. You don't have to attack me."

"I'm not attacking you, KC. I just want to

know what's going on. Believe it or not, I'm interested in what goes on inside that head of yours."

KC took a deep breath. "Okay. Well. I just don't . . . well, I don't feel very well." Instead of trying to hide her illness, she exaggerated her nasal voice and droopy eyes.

Peter stared at her again, then sat back. "Part of me wants to take this seriously, but I really don't think you're about to tell me you've got only six months to live."

"Of course I don't have only six months to live," she snapped.

"So what is it?"

KC couldn't quite put her thoughts in order. "I just . . . well, I don't know if I'll be able to go to Winter Formal after all. I have this cold and it seems like everyone in the dorms is getting sicker and sicker."

He smiled. "Not me."

"Peter, you know what I mean. I just don't know if it's really such a good idea to go. I don't know if I'll, well, feel up to it."

Peter thought for a moment. "So don't go," he said in an easy voice. "I haven't rented my tux yet or even bought the tickets. I thought we'd get them at the door. If you don't feel like going on Friday, we don't have to go."

As much as KC was relieved by Peter's casual attitude, she was also disappointed. *So don't go!* Why did an incredible guy like Warren seek her out, while ordinary Peter could take her or leave her? It was starting to make her crazy.

"You don't have to sound so blasé about it," she said. "*You* were the one who asked *me.* Matthew said you told him you were excited about going. I just didn't want to disappoint you if it didn't work out."

Peter was leaning forward now, brushing his hair away from his eyes and studying her. "Sure I'm excited about going, KC. But I get excited about going to the circus. I get excited about going home to see my kid brother, about taking pictures of tomatoes. That doesn't mean I'm going to kill myself if I find out those things aren't going to happen."

"Thanks a lot," KC exploded. "So going to Winter Formal with me ranks about as high as taking pictures of tomatoes!"

Peter held up his hands. "Whoa, KC. Look, I'd rather go to that dance with you than not go. If I hadn't wanted to go I never would have offered to take you. But it's no big deal. I don't know you all that well. It's just a way to spend a Friday night. Just because you're gorgeous doesn't mean that I think that going to a dance with you has to be the high point of my life."

KC's thoughts were a jumble. She wasn't sure if her cold was fogging up her head, or if it was her feelings that were making her so confused. "Well, maybe I want it to be a high point of my life, Peter. Maybe I want it to be exciting and special and extraordinary. And maybe that's why I'm not going with you, but I *am* going with someone else!"

Stunned surprise struck Peter's face. For a long time he sat silently, his mouth slightly open and his eyes full of anger. Finally he said, "Is that what you're trying to tell me, that you want to go to the dance with someone else?"

"I'm going with Warren Manning," KC boasted.

Peter let his head fall back. He almost laughed. "Well, that's perfect, KC. Just perfect. You said you'd go with me, and then you decide to back out because pretty Warren asked you instead."

"Can you blame me?"

Peter looked her straight in the eye and said coldly, "You bet I can blame you, KC. I can blame you for being fickle and inconsiderate and dumb."

KC stood up and started out. Her head was pounding and she wished that she could take every word that had come out of her mouth, erase them, and start over. "I should never have told you the truth. I should have known that you would just attack me."

"KC, what did you expect?" Peter asked. "You just treated me like dirt. Was I supposed to smile and say thank you?"

KC walked out and slammed Peter's door.

# Eleven

By Thursday, Faith had typed the lists posted on the walls of the U of S studio theater, the small "black box" theater where she was finally presenting her production of *Alice in Wonderland*. There were prop lists, costume lists, sign-in lists, and lists of music cues, lighting cues, entrances and exits.

And then there was the small list hidden away in the corner, written by hand, simply entitled "Faith's list." It said:

*Finish project for stagecraft class.*
*Check out Spanish language lab tapes.*

*Write Mom, Dad, and Marlee.*
*Do something about W and KC! Quick!*

Faith was staring at that list, thinking about her two best friends, when she felt a tap on her shoulder.

"Faith, Sara can't find her Alice apron," said Jacob Morganstern, a freshman who was running costumes. "Do you know where it is?"

Faith turned away from the backstage wall. "Did you check the laundry basket?"

Jacob looked embarrassed at forgetting to check such an obvious place. "No. Sorry. I bet it's there." He scurried away. A minute later he called back, "Thanks. I found it!"

Just then, Kimberly asked, "Faith, can I start the movement warmup now?"

Faith checked her watch. "Go ahead. I think everyone's here."

"Great." Kimberly put her hands to her mouth and hollered, *"Okay, everybody, let's start our warmup."*

"Faith," called out Rob Menendez, the actor who played the White Rabbit, "did the timing of that first rabbit-hole entrance work better yesterday?"

"It was perfect," Faith called back. "Do it exactly like that again today."

Next Faith heard Merideth, the stage manager, call from the back of the house, *"One hour to places, ladies and gentlemen. We start in one hour."*

Faith and her cast and crew were preparing for their second and final performance of *Alice in Wonderland,* Faith's independent-study project. The U of S studio theater was small and unpretentious, but it buzzed with excitement. Kimberly was leading the cast in a series of stretches while Sara, the little girl who played Alice, sat on the floor going over her lines with her mother. Crew members bustled around carrying hats and shoes, clipboards and notebooks. Lights were being tested and set pieces set up.

"And we finish in another hour and a half after that," Faith whispered. "All this work and it will be over so soon. Then it's back to reality."

Actually, Faith would welcome the return to reality. The first performance of *Alice in Wonderland* had gone brilliantly. Faith's independent-study advisor had come to watch, along with most of the important people from the theater-arts department. Faith had received so many compliments that she had barely been able to absorb them all. The small audience had laughed and gasped, even cried a little, and applauded like crazy. Suddenly everyone was referring to Faith as an up-and-coming director, one who had drive, imagination, and new ideas.

Stage manager Merideth hurried by, checking off a long list on his clipboard. "Have fun today," he told Faith. "This one's for free."

"I know," Faith sighed. "I can't believe it's almost over."

"Believe it." He smiled. "You did a great job."

Faith laughed.

The great job had taken all Faith's thought and energy. Meanwhile she'd pushed other important concerns out of her mind. But now that the play was almost over, Faith had to face the fact that she'd barely spoken to Lauren lately and didn't know what, if anything, had happened between Lauren and Dash. She had left classwork unfinished. And most important, she'd done nothing about the rift that had developed between Winnie and KC.

Faith walked over to the edge of the stage and looked out. There was no curtain in the studio theater, so she could peer right out at the audience, which at that moment consisted of rows of empty folding chairs. A few crumpled programs dotted the floor, and it looked like someone had forgotten a textbook at the first performance the day before.

Faith checked her watch again. She'd asked both KC and Winnie to come early and be ushers in the hope that they might talk to each other and begin to work things out. As Faith worried, the back door opened and KC strode in, wearing a velvet jacket, high-necked blouse, and pleated skirt. She carried herself stiffly, but looked as beautiful as ever.

Faith trotted out to greet her. "Hi, KC. Thanks for coming early to do this. I know you still have papers to finish."

KC shook her head. "I had to turn in my Western Civ paper this morning, finished or not. My English lit paper, too." She forced a smile. "I'm sure it will all be fine, though. I'll probably get more B pluses."

"Maybe you'll get an A plus." Faith noticed how uptight KC was, and began to wonder if KC was doing as well as she pretended. She was going to ask her about it when the door flew open a second time and Winnie bobbed in.

KC looked surprised to see Winnie. Her eyes turned hard and steely.

"Hello, campers." Winnie grinned. Josh was with her, holding her hand and leaning in to talk to her as they laughed their way up to meet Faith and KC. They were so obviously in love that just watching them made Faith blush.

"Hi, Win. Hi, Josh," Faith said.

KC stood tall and cool, barely acknowledging Winnie.

Meanwhile Winnie pretended not to notice KC and wrapped herself around Josh.

"Josh decided to come, too, Faith," Winnie chattered. "Mikoto wanted to take a nap and Josh was going to study in my room, but Melissa and Brooks had this fight and she's really mad at him, so she didn't exactly want Josh hanging out with her, so—" Winnie stopped for breath. "Here we are."

"Actually, I wanted to see your show," Josh said. "And I figured you could use another usher."

"You can never have too many ushers," said Faith. "Thanks a lot."

Josh smiled. "Winnie and I are going downtown afterward to get some last-minute stuff for Winter Formal. Do you want to come?"

"I can't," Faith answered. "I have to organize the cleanup. Anyway, I'm not going to Winter Formal. But maybe KC should go with you," Faith blurted, tapping into her old maternal, peacemaker streak. "KC, do you have your dress yet?"

"No. Until yesterday I was too busy with papers to shop," KC said coolly. "Then I finally went to all the department stores last night and I couldn't find anything I liked."

"KC," Faith reminded her, "the formal's tomorrow night. You'd better go and shop some more."

"I know!" KC tensed. "But I doubt that Winnie and I are planning to shop at the same places."

Winnie bristled, too. "I don't know where I'm going to shop today," she said, looking only at Faith. "Josh already has most of his stuff. I don't know what it is, though. We're meeting by the hotel swimming pool, like it's a blind date."

"So if you get something today, Win," Josh said, poking her in the ribs, "you can't let me see it."

Winnie nodded. "Right."

"KC," Faith insisted, "why don't you go with them? At least you can go downtown together." Faith wanted to push the issue even harder, but just then Merideth popped out from backstage.

"Faith, we need you a moment," Merideth interrupted. "Rob can't find his rabbit ears."

"I have to go," Faith said. She left Winnie and Josh smiling at each other while KC looked away and frowned.

"Maybe I'll wear a dinosaur suit with silver shoes."

"Winnie, don't tell me," Josh teased. "It has to be a surprise."

"Maybe we should plan one thing that will match, though."

Josh grinned. "Matching string ties."

"Matching spurs."

"Matching petticoats and big floppy skirts."

Winnie fell against Josh and laughed.

KC thought she was going to scream. She hadn't wanted to go with Winnie and Josh in the first place, yet here she was in the middle of Karlson's Western Wear while Winnie wasted valuable time trying on cowboy hats and making a spectacle of herself. The only reason KC had gone with them at all was that Faith had given her those don't-be-such-a-snob looks. Faith had a way of making KC feel that their old friendship was the most important thing in the world. Meanwhile, Faith could disappear backstage, leaving KC to hang out with flakey Winnie and hope that no one important came by and saw her.

Winnie and Josh began playing a game of keep-away with a tin of saddle soap. KC noticed the saleswoman glaring at them.

"Winnie, do you have to be so loud?" KC asked.

"KC, do you have to be so uptight?" Winnie tossed back before grabbing Josh around the waist and bursting into laughter again. Josh tickled Winnie and laughed, too.

KC couldn't stand it much longer. She couldn't stand wasting her time in Karlson's Western Wear when she had less than twenty-four hours to prepare for her date with Warren. She couldn't stand the fact that Winnie could leave everything to the last minute and still pull off As, while she worked and planned and ended up with Cs. And mostly she couldn't stand the fact that Winnie was so happy with Josh, while she had a date with the handsomest guy on campus but just felt angry and sad.

Josh tried on a huge cowboy hat, posing in front of the mirror while Winnie hung around his neck. "This is it, Win. I think you and I should dress as Roy Rogers and Dale Evans."

"Aren't they the people who stuffed their horse?" Winnie giggled.

"You just gave me an idea," Josh teased, leaning back to kiss Winnie's cheek. "I'll come as the stuffed horse." He kissed Winnie again, then went over to examine a rack of cowboy shirts.

With Winnie finally alone, KC said, "Entertaining as it is to watch you make a fool of yourself, Win, I have to go. I want to get down to The Strand, and most of the shops over there close at six."

Winnie turned and glared up at her. "Boring as it is to watch you act like Miss Uptight Sorority Queen, I don't care about the expensive shops on the exclusive Strand."

"Fine," KC stated angrily. "It wasn't my idea to come down here. Maybe we're carrying this old-friend thing a little too far. You and Josh do what you want. I'll just go on my way."

"You do that, KC," Winnie snapped. "Your way has always been so admirable. Like the way you told Peter you'd go to the formal with him, then changed your mind when somebody better-looking came along."

"Winnie." KC had told her about Warren and Peter while they'd ushered for *Alice in Wonderland*. She hadn't wanted to tell her, but there was no point in hiding the truth when she would just run into her at the dance. KC felt bad enough about the way she'd treated Peter without having Winnie throw it in her face. "You don't understand."

"I understand," Winnie came back. "I understand that none of us is good enough for you anymore. Not Peter Dvorksy and not me. And I understand that what you did was pretty low."

KC couldn't handle one more person telling her how thoughtless she was. "Well, is that any worse than you not telling Josh that Travis has been in town this whole time, even though you told Josh that Travis was gone?"

"What did you say?"

"You heard me, Win."

Winnie's mouth had fallen open and her eyes welled up with tears. She quickly looked around the store. At the same time both she and KC saw Josh. He was standing a few feet away, holding a cowboy shirt with guitars embroidered on the sleeves. His face had gone pale.

"Oh my God," Winnie whispered.

"Winnie, is that true?" Josh demanded, keeping his distance. "Is Travis still hanging around Springfield?"

"Um." Winnie stammered.

KC stared at the ground.

"Why did you lie to me? I thought we got past all that. I thought you were over him."

"I am!"

Josh shook his head. "Winnie." He began to back away from her. "I can't take this. I can't take this one-day-on, one-day-off stuff. I have to be able to trust you." Without another word, he turned and walked out of the store.

"Winnie, I'm sorry," KC breathed in a barely audible voice. She tried to backtrack, knowing that she'd done something terrible. "You told me that Josh knew about Travis."

"Of course he didn't know," Winnie cried. "You knew I was making that up."

"How could I know that?"

"You knew. For some reason you hate me these days."

"I don't hate you."

"You're embarrassed by me. But it's not enough for you just to snub me. You have to ruin my life, too!"

"Winnie, I didn't mean—"

"You meant every word." Winnie faced KC with wet, furious eyes.

"I'm sorry."

Tears ran down Winnie's face. "Sorry doesn't mean very much to me, KC."

"Win."

"You've hurt me plenty of times before and I've always forgiven you. But I can promise you, KC, I will never forgive you for this."

# Twelve

ou did a good job last weekend, Maureen."

"Thank you, Gladys."

"You work hard. You're polite. As head maid, I like that."

"Thanks."

"Now, your bed making is still a little sloppy, and you mixed up a few of your towel orders, but I'm sure you'll improve."

"I will."

"Where's your hat?"

Lauren touched her hair, which was already wilted from having eaten Friday-night dinner in the Springfield Mountain Inn's overheated kitchen. She was wearing her ridiculous uniform —poufy red skirt, apron, embroidered suspenders, and jogging shoes. She had intentionally left the absurd lace cap in her employee locker. "I must have forgotten my hat. I'm sorry."

Head maid Gladys Baker never seemed to forget anything. She was in her fifties, stocky and serious with gray hair arranged in a neat, netted bun. She held a clipboard. "Don't forget it again."

"I won't."

Gladys checked over her room chart. "This weekend looks a little slow on the upper floor, especially since that optometrists' convention left this morning." She sighed. "But we'll have to put up with all those college kids using the Powder Ballroom tonight."

"You mean the U of S Winter Formal."

"Winter whatever. All I know is that whenever we rent that ballroom out to those college kids, they mess up the whole first floor."

Lauren shrugged.

Gladys squinted at her list. "Why don't you work the laundry room tonight? Patty and I can take care of the upper floor."

"Okay." Spending the evening laundering endless piles of sheets and towels wasn't Lauren's idea of a great Friday night, but it was a step up from toilets and overflowing ashtrays.

"Have a nice shift," Gladys called as she pushed her cleaning cart and headed upstairs.

"You, too." Lauren walked down the long hall and around a corner, past the Downhill Breakfast Café and the Hot Spot disco. Just before sticking her key into the unmarked door that opened into the maids' laundry room, she heard the erratic twang of a band tuning up. She walked past the laundry room to look.

Sure enough, the music was coming from the Powder Ballroom. The band singer tested his mike, making jokes in between bursts of feedback that echoed and screamed.

"Winter Formal," Lauren sighed.

She peered into the lobby, then took a few steps closer to the Powder Ballroom, where she caught a glimpse of students making last-minute preparations. The first few couples were arriving, and Lauren saw silver-and-white decorations that reminded her of Christmas at her former Swiss boarding school. The band launched into a slow song. A girl laughed. For the first time Lauren felt a pang at missing Winter Formal.

Until that moment, she hadn't thought much

about the evening. She'd never had a boyfriend before Dash, so she'd never gone to formals or proms. But as much as she liked sitting home with a good book, something in her was also ready to dance the night away, to feel pretty and carefree. Something in her was ready to fall in love.

But as ready as Lauren may have been, that kind of night was not going to happen, she thought. Lauren knew it for certain when she caught sight of someone who gave her more than a pang. Seeing this person gave her an out and out heartache.

It was Dash. He was strolling through the lobby wearing his old leather jacket and baggy khakis. He was looking around, not in any kind of hurry.

Lauren wanted to run and shake him.

She didn't take a step.

She wanted to call out to him.

She didn't utter a word.

Lauren had already apologized when she'd seen him at the newspaper party a week earlier. She'd already explained that nothing had happened between her and Christopher Hammond. It was up to Dash to make the next move.

But Lauren hadn't heard a thing from Dash.

She didn't know much about guys, but even she could figure out what Dash was trying to say: *Get lost.*

"Hi, Dash," she whispered to herself. "Bye, Dash. I miss you, Dash."

Lauren stayed leaning against the wall as she watched Dash disappear around a corner. She thought about the strange turn her freshman year had taken. There were many things to be grateful for. She'd gotten away from the Tri Beta sorority. She'd taken a big step away from her overbearing mother. She'd done well on her exams, and her creative-writing teacher had said over and over that she had promise.

Of course, there had been disappointments and unexpected difficulties, too. But Lauren could handle being broke. She could handle changing sheets and washing people's dirty towels. She could even handle having a mother who bossed and manipulated her and a father who faded into the background.

What she couldn't handle, however, was that she'd gotten close to someone wonderful for a little while, and now she felt so out of place and lonely again.

* * *

"Well, would you look at that."

"What is it now, Marielle?"

"Maarrrk."

Mark imitated Marielle's expression and her whine. "Marielllllle."

Marielle punched him.

He touched his nose to hers.

"Look, Mark!"

"What am I looking at?" He put his hands on his cummerbund and shrugged. "A hallway?"

"That girl standing in the hallway."

"That's a maid, Marielle."

"I know it's a maid, Mark."

"Yeah. We're in a hotel. Hotels have maids."

"That's no ordinary maid." Marielle snickered. "That's Lauren Turnbell-Smythe. One of my pledges told me Lauren was working here, but I didn't believe it. Oh Mark, I wish I had a camera. This is too good to be true."

"I see what you mean." Mark guffawed. "The outfit is a nice touch. Maybe she'll be crowned freshman princess and get to start the last dance."

Marielle slugged him again and giggled. They were huddled in the Springfield Mountain Inn lobby, near the picture window that looked out onto the snow-capped mountains and dark forest. The icy moonlight filtered into the lobby area, which had thick, new carpet, furniture covered in pale velveteen, mirrored counters, and huge, delicate ferns. Ski Springfield! posters were hung on the peach-colored wallpaper.

Mark had rented a silk tuxedo with shiny black lapels and brocaded sleeves. It went perfectly with his dark mustache, and he looked like an elegant riverboat gambler who had just stepped ashore. Marielle knew that she looked good, too, in a floor-length black evening gown with spaghetti straps and a ruffle around the hem. When the bottom of her elegant dress swished across the floor, everyone took notice.

But for once, Marielle didn't want to be noticed. She and Mark had decided that this was their Get KC Angeletti Night. But since Courtney and a ton of other Tri Betas were in attendance at the dance, Marielle had to be careful. She had to be smart. She had to engineer her revenge just right.

Mark sat on the lobby sofa. He pulled Marielle down on his lap. "So should we get Turnbell-Smythe, too, while we're at it?" he whispered, nibbling at Marielle's ear.

Marielle curled up against him. She looked down the hall again, but Lauren was gone. "Too dangerous," she decided. "And not important enough. We can't get carried away."

"I like getting carried away, myself," Mark teased, nuzzling her.

Marielle jabbed him with her elbow, then noticed that a Tri Beta pledge was pointing at her and waving. Marielle stuck on a smile and waved back.

"What's the plan?" she muttered to Mark under her breath.

Mark tugged on his mustache. "I have to think about it. What do you want to accomplish?"

"We have to make KC do something embarrassing. But it won't be easy. She's here with Warren Manning. I've never known Mr. Beautiful or any girl he's ever been seen with to make a wrong move."

Mark huffed.

Marielle kept up her hushed instructions. "I just want to make sure KC doesn't win freshman princess. And I want Courtney to have to admit that I'm right, that KC Angeletti would be an embarrassment to the Tri Beta house."

Mark looked around.

Marielle paused to make sure that they weren't being overheard. "We can't do anything anywhere near the ballroom, because Courtney might see."

"Well, then, let's think of other places."

"Like where?"

Mark suddenly stood up, practically dumping Marielle off his lap. "We need some inspiration. Let's take a walk outside."

Marielle regained her balance in her high heels, then caught Mark's hand and accompanied him out of the lobby.

"It's cold out here," Marielle complained as soon as they passed through the lobby's double doors. It was dark, and frost hung in the air. Marielle shivered and held up her hand to shield her eyes from a car's headlights as it pulled into the lot. The car slowed down and a Tri Beta pledge stuck out her pretty head.

"Hi, Marielle. You look great," gushed the pledge, a freshman named Francia.

"So do you, Francia," Marielle sang back. As soon as the car rolled off and pulled into a space, Marielle leaned into Mark. "Did you ever see hair like that? I wonder where Francia got it done—the Reject Beauty College?"

Mark continued to wander and scout. More cars pulled into the lot.

"I don't know about you," Marielle complained, "but this is not giving me any good ideas. We need to find somewhere more private!"

"Stop talking, Marielle, and keep walking."

They continued to stroll, even though Marielle's teeth were chattering, her breath made clouds, and she had goosebumps up and down her arms. They wandered around the side of the inn until they found themselves in back of the indoor-pool area. An unfinished construction pit, surrounded by wheelbarrows, lengths of pipe, and sawhorses made them come to a stop. The asphalt had been dug up and the large hole was half filled with muddy water.

Mark walked away from her and examined the muddy pit. "It looks like they're starting to build saunas or something back here."

Marielle didn't follow him. The pit looked too dark, too wet, too gooey, and too disgusting. It was the size of a single dorm room and as deep as a wading pool.

They both lingered, standing a few feet apart, surveying the area. There were signs saying Construction Site and Keep Out. There was also a big pile of wood and concrete blocks to one side, which conveniently hid the healthy-sized hole from the view of the indoor-pool users.

"Are you thinking what I'm thinking?" Marielle grinned.

Mark came back over to her and slipped his arm over her bare shoulders. "How do you think a little mud bath would look before the crowning of the royal court?" Mark asked with a gleeful grin.

"Mud baths are good for the skin," Marielle gloated. "I'll just have to figure out some way to get KC out here. Meanwhile, you can be back here waiting for her."

"So you think this is it?"

"I think this is it." Marielle stood up on tiptoe and kissed Mark's mouth. "KC helped drag you through the mud. Now it's time for you to return the favor."

# Thirteen

People applauded. Flash bulbs went off. Out of the corner of her eye, KC saw even Marielle Danner watching her, staring with what KC could only interpret as envy.

"KC, get on my right side," Warren whispered.

"What?"

"On my right, please." Without dropping his dazzling smile, Warren gently shifted KC from his left arm to his right. "My right side is better for photographs. Smile."

"I'm smiling."

KC and Warren were making a fashionably late

entrance, stepping under the Winter Formal's royal arch, a structure near the entrance to the Powder Ballroom that was covered with white flowers, glitter, and satin bows. As students passed through the arch their picture was taken and they were formally entered into the competition for winter court.

Warren tipped his face toward the camera, offering first a smile, then a sleepy-eyed, sexy look. KC blinked as the flashbulb went off. The photographer kept shooting, taking at least twice as many shots of them as he'd taken of any other couple. The popping brightness gave KC a headache. She was loaded up with cold medicine, which had stopped her runny nose but left her with a cotton mouth and dry, itchy eyes. But that wasn't the only reason she felt so uncomfortable. Her head ached with regrets over how she'd treated Peter and Winnie.

KC froze until Warren guided her through the floral arch and over to a long table decorated with lilies. At the table, she and Warren signed official winter-court entry forms.

"I'm Carol," bubbled the girl who was behind the court registration desk. "I'm from the U of S social-activities committee."

"Warren Manning," said Warren with his winning smile. "And this beautiful woman is KC Angeletti."

Carol smiled at KC, then stared at Warren and blushed. "Warren Manning, you go in the senior pile. Do you understand how winter court is chosen?"

"I believe so, but why don't you tell me?" Warren said, keeping his arm snugly around KC.

"I will." Carol giggled. "We have a committee of former court members. You can see who they are, because they all spend the first half of the dance observing the contestants." Carol pointed. "The committee members can walk around to observe, but they also have seats set up against the far wall. Their decisions are based on how people present themselves at the dance. So it's important to make a good impression."

KC looked at the far wall, where most of the committee members were seated. There was only one committee member that KC recognized: Tri Beta president Courtney Conner. KC took a deep breath.

"Midway through the dance," Carol continued, "the committee will get together and decide on this year's court. The winners will be announced at exactly ten o'clock. Good luck."

"Thank you," said Warren.

Carol leaned over her table. "Um, this is kind of embarrassing, but I have my U of S calendar in my bag. Would you sign your picture for me?"

Warren's smile widened. He straightened the little red tie that perfectly set off his black cutaway. "Of course."

KC watched Warren sign "To Carol. Sincerely, Warren." Then he checked his face in the mirror behind Carol's head and seemed to practice his sultry smile.

"You're in the calendar, too, aren't you?" Carol asked KC.

KC nodded.

"Your photo is spectacular."

KC knew that Carol didn't want her autograph, so she moved away from the table and checked herself out in the mirror as well. At the last minute she'd found a dress at Fredericka's on The Strand. It was a long-sleeved, low-cut gown that hugged her body and left her shoulders bare. It had been on sale, but even so it had cost KC nearly every penny she had earned from the sales of the U of S calendar.

"Let's take a look at you, KC," Warren suddenly said, adjusting his collar and taking a deep breath. He put his hands on KC's shoulders and looked into her eyes.

KC looked back into Warren's cover-model face and tried to find something important there, something interesting. She didn't know Warren very well. Their few conversations up until that point had been about what time he was going to pick her up and what they were going to wear. Even their earlier chat that evening had been about cummerbunds and cuff links, weather and hair. KC had been hoping to get to know Warren, to meet the person under the handsome face.

"You look great," Warren said, touching KC's cheek. "I knew you would."

"You look great, too."

"I love your dress."

"I like your tux." KC's mind began to wander. She was gazing into Warren's eyes, but her thoughts were still on Winnie and Peter. She also noticed that Marielle Danner and Mark Geisslinger were still staring at her. KC shifted to avoid Marielle's gaze.

Warren looked past KC and studied his reflection in the mirror again. "Do I look sunburned?"

"What?"

"Do you think I got a sunburn?"

"Sunburn?" KC had to wonder why Warren would be concerned with sunburn in early January. "Are you a skier?" she asked vaguely. "I didn't know there was enough snow yet to go skiing on Wimer Mountain."

"I'm not interested in skiing," Warren told her.

"Oh?" KC forced herself to conjure up more exotic ways of getting a winter sunburn: mountain climbing, studying the rare plants on Golden Peak, hiking to the top of Springfield Butte to contemplate the universe. She tried to convince herself that Warren wasn't just a pretty face, that he was brave and intelligent and deep.

"I used the sun lamp at a new health club downtown," Warren confessed, still checking himself out in the mirror. "I think the bulb was stronger than what I'm used to. I hope I don't peel."

"Ugh. I hope not, too."

Warren cautiously touched his chin.

KC led the way toward the dance floor. She looked around for Marielle and Mark, but they were gone. Instead, she noticed another photographer, reloading film. Unlike the professional photographer under the arch, who'd been wearing a tux and would try to sell their photos to them later on, this photographer was scruffily dressed and looked bored. He was standing with another guy who wore jeans, needed a shave, and had a leather jacket slung over his shoulder. The second guy was writing notes on a small pad and looked even more bored than his photographer friend.

"That's Dash Ramirez," KC said.

"Who?"

"He's a friend of a friend of mine. He works for the *U of S Weekly Journal.* I don't really know him, but from what I've heard, he's an interesting guy."

Dash looked up and seemed to recognize KC. He waved and walked over.

"Hi. You're a friend of Lauren's, aren't you?" Dash said to KC, not even noticing Warren.

KC nodded.

"Is Lauren here tonight?" Dash's dark eyes looked confused and a little sad. "She said she worked here on weekends. I looked for her upstairs where they were cleaning the rooms, but I didn't see her. Do you know where she is?"

"Sorry, I don't," KC answered. "What are you doing here?"

Dash shrugged. "The paper wanted somebody to cover this. I only took the job because I thought I might run into Lauren. Hey, do you want your picture taken for the paper? I guess we should take a picture of somebody."

"Sure—"

"No thank you," Warren intruded, grabbing KC's arm. "Newspaper photos are always grainy and out of focus. And we're not just somebody."

"Sorry," Dash sighed.

"No, *I'm* sorry," KC whispered.

Warren was already steering her onto the dance floor. "Come on, KC," he urged. "It's time to make our appearance before the committee. Let's let them take a good look, because I know they're going to like what they see."

Winnie hadn't bothered with her special Winter Formal outfit. She'd left her poodle skirt back in her dorm room, along with her thrift-store fur and the bustier she'd dyed bright pink. What was the point of bothering with some wild outfit when she didn't even know if Josh was going to show up?

Wearing running tights and an old sweater, Winnie sat at the edge of the inn's swimming pool with her footless tights rolled up and her jingle-bell boots off. She dangled her feet in the warm water and looked at the condensation clinging to the walls. She breathed in the smell of chlorine and mildew and rubbed her eyes, which were red from crying.

"Please show up, Josh. Please."

Winnie held on to some small, impossible hope that Josh might still show up for their "blind date." She didn't know how else to find him, since he hadn't been back to the dorm since KC had blurted out that Travis was still in town. Winnie had even gone down her hall at four that morning and banged on Josh's door. But the only thing she'd accomplished was waking Mikoto up and finding out that Josh had spent the whole night somewhere else.

"Where?" Winnie cried softly. She lifted her foot out of the water, then kicked violently, making a loud splash. She wondered if Josh had tried to get back at her by spending the night with another girl.

*How could I blame him?* she thought, cursing herself for ever being anything but totally upfront. What was wrong with her, anyway? Why did she take the best guy she had ever known and mess everything up? And why had KC made the mess so much messier?

"I hate you, KC," Winnie grumbled. She looked back toward the ballroom and listened to the muffled music, barely audible over the hum of the pool filter. The air was so hot and thick that Winnie was beginning to feel dizzy. Steam rose off the pool, giving the whole place a blurry, surrealistic feel. Winnie thought of throwing herself in the water. She was picturing herself on the bottom of the swimming pool when she heard a door swing open.

She stood up in her bare feet and gasped. It was Josh. He had shown up after all.

Winnie started to run toward him, then stopped herself when she saw who was standing next to him. It wasn't another girl. It was even worse than that. Travis Bennett was standing by Josh's side.

"Travis."

"Hi, beautiful."

"Hello, Win," said Josh.

The sight of Josh and Travis standing there together was so unexpected that Winnie almost thought she was hallucinating. Travis looked intense, while Josh looked thoughtful. The two guys stepped a little closer, through the steam and the heavy air. They stared at her.

Winnie wondered if Josh and Travis had run into each other by accident, but when she looked at them closely, she saw anger in both of their faces.

"You were right," Travis said to Josh in a tired voice. "She's here."

"I thought she would be."

"Man, maybe you do know her better than I do," Travis replied.

"I doubt that," said Josh. "You've known her since last summer."

"Yeah. I guess we have more background together, but you go to college with her. I'm into a whole different thing."

"Yeah."

Winnie continued staring at them and began to shiver. She got a horrible feeling in the pit of her stomach. Somehow Josh and Travis had become friends—and they were united against her.

"Josh, where were you last night?" Winnie asked, hoping to put Josh on the defensive.

Josh glanced at Travis. "Win, I finally decided to find out what was going on with you. It didn't seem like you were being straight with me, so I went to the Beanery and talked to Travis. I didn't have any other choice. Travis and I stayed up late talking and I slept on his floor."

"We talked a lot, Win," Travis confirmed. "It was very interesting."

Winnie wanted to sink into the concrete.

"It seems that each of us was under the impression that he was the only one," Josh said. "Travis may be about to leave town, but you didn't tell him that things between you and him were over."

"And you never told me about this other dude, Win," Travis said. "From the way Josh tells it, things between the two of you are pretty heavy."

Winnie stared back and forth, from Josh to Travis. Travis was the first guy she'd ever loved. Josh was the guy she loved now. Even though she knew that Travis was part of her past and Josh was her present and future, seeing them together made her feel out of kilter. Her motor mouth was out of gas. She could barely breathe. She just stood there, staring at them, unable to say a word.

"So what we decided," Travis said, "was that we'd come here together and face you and make you tell us which one you really want to be with."

"That way," Josh agreed, "we'll both finally know the truth and we can get on with our lives."

"You decided," Winnie repeated. "*You* decided!"

They both nodded.

"The gig is up, beautiful," Travis warned.

"That's right, Win. Which one of us is it going to be?"

Winnie felt as if she were drowning after all. She knew that there was no longer any way to win. Of course, Josh was the guy she wanted now, but part of her still loved Travis, too, and still appreciated the kindness he'd shown her in Paris and the devotion he'd shown after so much time apart. She realized that the reason she hadn't told Travis about Josh was that she hadn't wanted to hurt him—to dump him—the way that so many guys had hurt her. Even now, she couldn't look Travis in the face and tell him that she was in love with Josh.

"I won't choose with both of you here in front of me. Don't make me do that. I can't."

"Either choose or we both walk," said Travis.

Josh nodded.

Winnie's brain was stopped up. She couldn't do it. It was too cruel, too crass, too much like the awful things that guys had done to her. She couldn't hurt Travis, even if it meant losing Josh.

"I can't choose," she whispered. "I won't do it. It doesn't work like that."

Travis and Josh looked at each other. They each took a deep breath. Then, as if by former agreement, they turned and left the hotel.

After they were gone, Winnie stood staring at

her reflection in the water, not knowing what to do. She kicked her boots.

"KC, this is all your fault," Winnie sobbed. "I know it's my fault, too, but how could you have done it? You were supposed to be my best friend!"

# Fourteen

C was being watched.

Courtney Conner was only a few feet away, smiling at KC as she roamed the dance floor and made notes in a little book. Other dancers gawked at KC and Warren as if they were movie stars. Even Marielle Danner, gliding in Mark Geisslinger's arms, stared at KC and studied her.

"That's one more judge in our corner," Warren whispered as he led KC in a graceful two-step. The band was playing a forties medley, led by a singer who crooned like Linda Ronstadt.

"Who?"

"The Grace Kelly blonde." Warren guided his hand along KC's back so that she could see Courtney give a little wave. Courtney held up an okay sign, then backed away.

"How do you know she's in our corner?" KC asked after Courtney had disappeared into the crowd.

Warren gently put his cheek against hers, but he didn't nuzzle or caress or kiss her. KC wondered if he was worried about messing up his hair.

"I can tell about these things," Warren assured her. "Just like I knew you'd break your other date and come to this dance with me."

KC's head began to pound. She wondered if the cold medicine was wearing off, or if she was getting even sicker.

Warren twirled her, then pulled her in again. "You're a good dancer."

"No, I'm not." Usually KC was a terrible dancer. Warren just knew how to lead so that they looked great together. And yet, in spite of the way they looked, KC felt as if she were dancing with a robot.

Warren slid his hand around her waist in a studied embrace. They kept on dancing. Other couples moved away to make room for them.

People pointed and whispered. KC held back a sneeze.

Later KC felt a tap on her shoulder and, for the first time that evening, she stepped on Warren's toe. She had a flashback to high school and guys cutting in. Suddenly she daydreamed that Peter Dvorsky had realized that he was impressed by her after all, and that he had run out of his dorm room, raced through the cold, and burst his way into the Springfield Mountain Inn to push Warren away and claim her.

*What am I thinking?* KC asked herself. She had never been one to indulge in such lame, syrupy fantasies, especially about ordinary guys like Peter.

"KC," said a female voice from behind KC's right shoulder.

The tap on her shoulder was repeated. This time KC felt the pressure of a long fingernail and caught a glimpse of bright red polish.

"Yes?" KC stopped dancing. She wondered why Marielle was approaching her. "Marielle. Do you know Warren?"

"I know who Warren is," Marielle flirted. "I think everyone does."

Warren smiled.

"Where's Mark?" KC asked politely.

Marielle seemed flustered for a moment. "Oh . . . he just . . . went outside to get some air."

"That's nice."

Marielle smiled. KC wondered if she wanted to dance with Warren, but Marielle's eyes stayed on KC. "KC, Courtney asked me to tell you that she'd like to talk to you privately. I guess it's very important."

"Really?" KC's heart picked up. Maybe all the pain and sacrifice of the last few days would be worth it after all. Maybe Courtney wanted her to know that she was a shoo-in for freshman princess and for membership in the Tri Betas. "Do you know what Courtney wants to talk to me about?"

It took a second for Marielle to answer. "I don't," she said. "But I expect it has something to do with winter court."

"What did I tell you?" Warren grinned.

Marielle gestured toward the ballroom exit. "Courtney is waiting for you on the other side of the inn. You just walk through the indoor pool area to get there. I guess that was the only quiet place she could find to talk to you. I'll take you there."

KC glanced up at Warren. "Do you mind if I go and talk to Courtney for a few minutes?"

"Not at all. I think it's a good idea." Warren looked smug. "Go ahead. I'll talk to a few more judges here and meet you near the arch when you get back."

KC smiled at Warren, then followed Marielle out of the ballroom.

"My life is a mess. It's a total, complete mess."

Winnie didn't know what to do or where to go. She'd wandered down the halls of the inn. She'd rushed into the bathroom, but then realized that it was full of girls gossiping about who was going to win winter court. She'd even stepped into the Hot Spot disco until she'd been ordered out for being underage. Part of her wanted to go back to the dorm, but part of her was too hysterical to leave the inn. Part of her was also aware that it was freezing out and she wasn't wearing shoes.

Out of sheer frustration, Winnie beat on the next door she saw, an unmarked beige slab of steel that she figured opened onto a broom closet. She was totally stunned when the door swung open and a familiar face appeared.

"Lauren!" Winnie cried.

"Winnie." Lauren opened the door further and led Winnie into a small cubicle filled with washers and dryers, shelves lined with soap and bleach, an ironing board, and a mountain of dirty linen. It was hot and hard to hear over the rumble of the machines.

"I'm so glad I found you," Winnie said. "I think you're my only friend."

"What are you talking about, Win? You have the two best friends in the world."

Winnie shook her head. "All Faith cares about lately is the theater-arts department. And KC just did it to me again!"

"What are you talking about? What did KC do?"

Winnie began to weep. "She told Josh about Travis and now they both hate me. Josh and I are over. KC ruined my life. I can't believe she wanted to hurt me like that."

Lauren sat Winnie down.

"Remember what KC did to you?" Winnie wailed, her grief turning to anger. "I should have known when she helped set you up for that fraternity prank that I never should have trusted her again. I'll never trust her now, that's for sure. Why did you ever forgive her?"

Lauren held Winnie's shoulders, trying to calm

her down. "Sometimes it's better to forgive people, Winnie. Sometimes they make mistakes and they do dumb things, but they deserve a second chance."

"I'll never give KC a second chance," Winnie railed.

"Winnie, calm down."

"I won't calm down!" Winnie pulled away from Lauren. "I'm so angry and upset that I don't know what to do!"

Lauren held Winnie for a while as a washer spun and Winnie's tears turned to shudders. Finally Winnie turned away from her.

Lauren walked across the tiny room and lifted the curtain on a small window that looked out onto the indoor-pool area. "Win, have you seen Dash? I thought I saw him go into the ballroom."

"I never made it into the ballroom. I just sat by that pool, waiting, and then Josh and Travis showed up looking like they were best buddies. I feel like I didn't do anything wrong, and like I did everything wrong. All I know is that I'll never forgive KC. And I can't find my shoes."

Lauren stood up on tiptoe, still looking out the little window. "You mean your boots with the jingle bells?"

Winnie sniffed and nodded.

"They're out by the pool, Win. I can see them from here."

Winnie stopped sniffling. After rubbing watery mascara around her puffy face, she joined Lauren at the window and looked out. "Oh yeah. There they are." She continued to stare, still letting out little weepy moans. Then she gasped. "My boots aren't the only things hanging out by that stupid pool."

Lauren saw what Winnie was referring to. KC had just entered the pool area. Not wanting Winnie to go into her tirade again, Lauren tried to guide her away from the window.

Winnie refused to budge. "I can barely stand to look at KC," she raved. "Oh, I don't believe it. Will you look at who's walking in behind her?"

"Who?"

"She's with Marielle Danner."

"You're kidding."

"No. Oh, this is perfect. Just perfect." Winnie suddenly bolted away from the window and back over to the laundry-room door.

"Where are you going?" Lauren asked as Winnie pushed the door open and started to run out into the hall.

"I'm going to get my boots," Winnie barked. "And to show KC exactly what I think of her."

"We're almost there, KC. Just follow me past the diving board."

"I'm following, Marielle." KC tiptoed around the chaises longues, the lifeguard chair, and the stacks of kickboards. Water lapped the sides of the pool, and she wondered if the humid air was smudging her makeup or frizzing her hair. She lifted the hem of her dress and stepped over damp tile and concrete.

Wearing a sly smile, Marielle beckoned her toward the back door of the pool area. She put her hand on the knob, then tensed. "It's locked," Marielle said with a panicked look.

KC was starting to get a funny feeling. She'd never been quite sure how to read Marielle. She certainly didn't trust her and she was beginning to think that something strange might be in the works.

"Wait right here," Marielle instructed. "Don't move. I'm just going to find another way to get out there. I'll be right back."

"Hurry up, Marielle."

"KC, this was Courtney's idea, not mine. She said it was important."

"All right. I'll wait." KC didn't like the idea of being away from the dance floor and the judges for so long.

Marielle scampered away. "I'll be back in two seconds," she called back. "Don't go anywhere."

The door flapped open and closed, then open and closed again. KC wondered if Marielle had come right back in, but she didn't look back because she was distracted by the sight of something else. A pair of lavender boots with jingle bells were by the edge of the swimming pool. KC recognized them instantly as Winnie's boots and suddenly she wanted to cry.

"Why don't you just kick them in the water?" Winnie said, bitterly. "You've already kicked *me* around."

KC spun around at the sound of Winnie's voice. She couldn't believe that Winnie was there, and that her friend had such fury in her voice and such a wild look in her eyes. KC moved back, nearer to the edge of the pool. "Winnie, I want to talk to you. I didn't know if you had come to the formal after all."

"Oh, I'm here, KC," Winnie raged. "I'm here. That's one thing you won't forget for a long time, the fact that I was here."

"Win."

Winnie's eyes were glazed with anger. KC tried to get out of the way, but she couldn't maneuver in time. Before she knew it, Winnie rushed at her with arms outstretched and gave her a big shove. Suddenly there was nothing under KC's feet and a moment later her entire body was surrounded by warm water.

*"Winniieeeee!"*

KC tried to take a breath and swallowed chlorinated water. She flailed and flapped her arms. When she popped to the surface she coughed and splashed. It suddenly felt as if her nose were about to run down her face. Her dress stuck to every part of her, and as she paddled to the side of the pool she could already feel the material stretching out of shape. Through stinging eyes, she looked up at Winnie, who was still standing at the edge of the pool.

Winnie looked stunned, as if she couldn't believe what she'd done either. "Oh my God."

*"What did you do?"* KC screamed. She dog-paddled over to the side and pulled herself up. As she looked down at her drenched body, KC started to cry. "What am I going to do now?" She tried to pull the bottom of her dress from under her feet, but tripped backward and fell right back in the water.

Just then another set of footsteps quickly traveled across the concrete. KC looked up. It was Marielle, staring down at KC with an expression of confusion and utter disbelief.

*"Don't just stare at me,"* KC screamed. *"Somebody do something!"*

Winnie began to weep.

Marielle seemed paralyzed. She stared at KC as if she'd seen a ghost. KC wasn't sure if Marielle was pleased or outraged.

Finally Marielle got a pensive look, then a smile on her face. She took a step forward and extended a manicured hand to KC. "I'll help you, KC," Marielle purred. "It's about time you found out who your real friends are."

KC let Marielle pull her out of the pool. She wouldn't even look at Winnie as she and Marielle stumbled away.

# 

"All right, I'm a jerk."

"You're a jerk."

"I'm overprotective."

"You are."

"Melissa, you don't have to agree with me on everything."

"*You* said it, Brooks, not me."

While most of his friends were dancing at the Winter Formal, Brooks sat in the dank U of S weight room under banks of harsh fluorescent lights. He didn't mind the glare or the smell. At that moment the gym was more appealing to him than any fancy ballroom because Melissa was sitting on the weight bench next to him.

"I was only overprotective because I care so much about you," he explained.

Melissa looked down. She slowly tugged off her leather lifting gloves. "I know that, too."

"And you're not exactly an easy person to take care of. Getting you to admit that you might need help is about as easy as getting an A plus in honors chem."

Melissa cracked a tiny smile.

"So how are you feeling? If it's okay to ask," Brooks said, nudging her. "I've missed you for the last few days."

"I'm fine."

"Really fine, or Melissa fine?"

"Really fine." She nudged him back. "I've missed you, too. I've been a royal grump since we had that fight. Winnie kept trying to talk to me and I was like a stone."

"Poor Winnie."

The only other athletes in the weight room, two bulky football players, packed up their gear and left. After they had gone, it was quiet.

"Look, I'm sorry I blew up and just left," Melissa finally admitted.

"It would have been better if you'd stuck around so we could have kept talking."

"You're right. But you know how defensive I can be."

He smiled. "I know. I thought we were working on that."

Melissa laughed softly. "Yeah. Well, maybe we should work on your overprotectiveness, too. Maybe we can make a trade."

"Okay." Brooks sighed. "Actually, I've been thinking about this a lot over the last few days."

"And?"

Brooks took a deep breath. "When Faith and I were together I always felt as if I had to protect her, and that's what wrecked things between us." He turned and took Melissa's hands. "I don't want to wreck things with you, Mel."

She bit her lip. "I don't either."

They looked into each other's eyes, but just as they were about to kiss, the gym manager poked his head in.

"We're closing up," the manager announced. "Time to go home." He started turning off the banks of lights.

Brooks stood up, then pulled Melissa up, too. "Come on. Let's go back to the dorms. All those people at Winter Formal may think they're having a great time, but it's nothing compared to sitting in the dorm TV room, eating popcorn and watching old Star Trek reruns."

Melissa put on her parka and led the way to the exit. "Sounds like a great time to me."

"Wear my dress, KC."

"I can't wear your dress, Marielle."

"Well, you can't wear your own dress. Even if we stuck it in Lauren's dryer, it would still come out looking like something from the black lagoon. Right, Lauren?"

"It probably would," Lauren confirmed.

"So put on my dress," Marielle repeated. "I think we're the same size."

"But Marielle, what will you wear?"

"I can just wrap myself in one of these hotel bathrobes and sneak home."

"I could do that, too."

"KC," Marielle lectured, "you have a good chance at winter court. More than a good chance. No one cares if I disappear tonight. But you will be missed."

KC toweled her limp, wet hair and looked at Lauren.

Lauren shrugged.

"I'm right," Marielle insisted. "You know I'm right." She began to slither out of her expensive gown and tried not to get distracted. From the Springfield Mountain Inn maids' laundry room, Marielle was keeping track of a lot of different things. How long she had to get KC ready for the crowning of the winter court. How patiently Mark would wait outside by the construction pit before realizing that there had been a change in plans. Whether KC, who was smart and quick, would be desperate enough to trust her.

"Where did Winnie go?" KC asked. She had begun to shiver. Her nose was running a little and her eyes looked glassy.

Lauren peered through the little window that looked out onto the pool. "She was too upset to stay. After Marielle brought you back here, she left. I think she took a cab back to the dorms."

"Nice of her to say goodbye," KC grumbled.

"She was crying."

"Forget it," KC decided. "I'm never speaking to her again. I just wish Faith were here. Maybe now she wouldn't think that everything was my fault."

"I could call Faith," Lauren volunteered.

"Don't bother," KC grumbled. "She's probably busy with some new play."

"Why don't you let me handle this?" Marielle said, covering her dislike of Lauren with a sweet smile. She was glad that KC was suddenly on the outs with her two best friends. That gave her even more of an opportunity. "I'll take care of everything."

Lauren narrowed her eyes.

KC looked confused.

Marielle ignored Lauren's reaction. "Don't worry, KC."

Marielle had a brand-new plan that covered every angle. This opportunity had fallen into her lap thanks to great luck, quick thinking, and impulsive Winnie Gottlieb. At first Marielle had been stunned and outraged that Winnie had gotten to KC ahead of her. But then she'd realized that Winnie had created an even better opening for her. If Marielle couldn't be the one to humiliate KC, then she could step in to save her instead. She could get close to KC, waiting patiently until a much richer and more rewarding moment arrived to get her revenge. It was such a delicious plan that Marielle had to remind herself not to giggle out loud.

"What about my hair?" KC asked.

"I can borrow a blow dryer from the pool dressing room," Lauren suggested.

Marielle subtly shoved Lauren aside. "There's no need for that. Look, the judging has already taken place. It's just your appearance at the crowning that matters now."

"Assuming I win."

"Even if you don't win, KC, you don't want to leave early. That just makes you look like a bad sport. And what about Warren?"

KC didn't answer.

Lauren went back to folding towels.

"My point is," Marielle went on, "that everyone will know you're wearing a different dress. That will be all too obvious."

"They'll know I'm wearing *your* dress."

"They won't know that it's my dress. Luckily I keep a low profile at things like this," Marielle said with false modesty. "What we have to do is make them think that you intentionally changed your clothes because you have such a fabulous sense of style. It'll be your statement. If you carry this off with enough confidence, next year every girl will be changing her dress midway through Winter Formal."

KC rubbed her eyes. "Lauren, what do you think?"

Lauren hesitated.

"And that's why we don't want a blow dryer," Marielle went on quickly. "I think we should do something radically different with your hair, too.

How about keeping it wet and slicking it back off your neck and face? Then we can put lots of dark eye makeup on you, plus a little bit of lipstick. You'll look spectacular."

"I doubt that," KC groaned.

"Trust me." Marielle wrapped herself in a Springfield Mountain Inn bathrobe and slipped her dress over KC. She turned KC around, zipped the zipper, then cooed with delight. "It fits. You look fabulous. This dress looks better on you than it does on me."

KC showed herself to Lauren. "Lauren, does it look okay?"

"It looks great on you," Lauren whispered. She glanced at Marielle, then turned back to her sheets and towels.

Marielle put her hands on KC's shoulders and sat her down on an old wooden chair. She opened her beaded shoulder bag and dumped out the contents. Makeup, brushes, mints, and a tiny container of hair mousse spilled out.

"Close your eyes and hold still," Marielle ordered.

KC held her breath as Marielle sculpted and brushed. After everything that had happened, she was a sitting duck. Even if Marielle had been painting orange flames across her nose, KC wouldn't have moved. Her head hurt. Her eyes stung. Her heart was sore with the thought that she had just lost one of her best friends as well as Peter. And she didn't know what to think about winter court or Warren, who probably thought she'd run off with a bellhop.

"Done. You look great," Marielle said after applying more eyeliner and blush. She opened her compact and held it in front of KC.

KC looked in the mirror. She expected to see herself made up like Bozo the clown, but that wasn't the case. She looked different—exotic and chic.

"What do you think?" Marielle asked.

KC stood up, her courage finally returning. She was beginning to think that maybe she could face Warren, Courtney, and the rest of the ballroom crowd after all. "I look good," she whispered.

Marielle gave her a little hug. "Of course you do." She kicked off her shoes. "Slip these on and get going. It's almost time to announce the court. I didn't go through all this work to have you sit back here and watch Lauren fold sheets."

Lauren flinched.

KC let Marielle lead her out of the laundry room and into the hall.

"Go on. I can't go with you in this bathrobe. I'll call you later tonight, to see how it went."

"Thanks." Feeling as if she were in a dream, KC left Marielle. Maybe water was still in her ears or the cold was going to her brain, but she felt as if she were floating down the hotel hallway, cruising on air as the music from the ballroom got louder and louder. By the time she reentered Winter Formal, she was wearing a beatific smile.

Warren rushed over to her as soon as she neared the arch. "Where were you? It's time to announce the court."

"It's a long story."

When he took a good look at her, his annoyance turned to approval. "Oh. You changed your whole look. Why didn't you tell me you were going to do that? I would have done it, too." He slipped his arm around her. "What a great idea. You look even better than you did before."

KC wasn't sure how to reply, but she didn't have to say anything because just then the band stepped out of the limelight. Courtney and the rest of the previous year's winter court took the stage.

The outgoing senior queen stepped up to the mike. "It's wonderful to be back at Winter Formal," she said graciously. "You all know why I'm standing up here, so I won't keep you waiting too much longer. We'll start with freshman princess. The winner is . . . KC Angeletti!"

When KC heard her name, she felt her head clear and her spirits soar. Thoughts of Winnie and Peter faded away as she stepped up onto the stage. People cheered and the professional photographer snapped more pictures. KC smiled down at Warren. Courtney took a step forward to pat her shoulder and give her a smile.

*Thank you, Marielle,* KC said to herself. *Thank you.*

Hotel blues.

That's what Dash had. He tried to focus his attention on the court that was being crowned, but he hadn't observed much of the Winter Formal so far, and the high point of the dance didn't capture his interest, either. He told himself that this was a job and that he had an article to write. And yet, the longer he stood in the Powder Ballroom, the more he thought about Lauren and how much he missed her. Only Lauren's presence would have made the occasion something special.

"Take a walk, Ramirez," Dash finally told himself. He walked behind the crowd, which was enthralled by the announcement of Warren Manning as senior king. Grabbing a cup of punch on his way out, Dash told himself that he should give his story another try.

But he wasn't in the mood. So he pushed the back door open.

"Oh."

"Hey."

"Hi."

"You're here after all."

"I'm here."

There she was on the other side of the door, peeking in. Dash wanted to take her in his arms and never let go.

"Did KC win?" Lauren asked.

"Yes." Dash slipped outside and let the door close. He stood with Lauren in the hall. There was another burst of applause from inside the ballroom. "She won easily."

"Good. I guess."

Dash couldn't take his eyes off her. Her uniform made him want to laugh, but otherwise she looked great.

Lauren finally lowered her eyes. "I'm done with my shift."

"Oh, that's right. You were working tonight."

"I just wanted to find out if KC had won."

"Well, she did."

"Yeah. You told me."

"Oh. Yeah."

They stood in the hall for another minute and then, at the same time, they both began to walk. Dash wondered if they would stroll through the lobby and out the front door, not even bothering to say goodnight, as if they barely knew each other. They kept walking. Step, step, step. It was going to happen. They were both going to be too proud to take advantage of what was probably their last chance.

They approached the lobby and Lauren walked faster. Dash felt the breeze from her red skirt as she passed him by. She was getting farther ahead of him, almost out of reach. Then, at the last second, he let down his tough exterior and reached out, catching her hand just before she got too far away.

She stopped.

Dash pulled her in.

He'd only meant to get her attention, to say hello, to look at her one last time and memorize the incredible violet color of her eyes.

But he was kissing her instead. Or maybe she was kissing him. Dash wasn't sure who had started it and he didn't care, because his head was spinning and her lips were soft and he wanted to keep standing there, kissing her forever.

"Hi," she whispered, her eyes filling with tears when at last they drew apart.

"Hi," Dash breathed, throwing his arms around her again and embracing her for a long time.

"I missed you, Dash."

"I missed you. I missed you like crazy."

They began to laugh.

Lauren took a step toward the door. "Are you coming with me or do you have to stay and cover the dance?"

"I'm sure not letting you walk away."

They stood gazing at each other.

"Maybe we should go back into the ballroom," Dash suggested suddenly.

"I always wanted to go to a Winter Formal," Lauren confessed.

"Do you want to?"

"Do you?"

"I don't know."

"I'm not really dressed . . ."

"Well, look at me."

Dash grabbed Lauren's hand and the two of them ran back toward the ballroom to dance the night away.

# Sixteen

On Sunday the first big snow came to Springfield. Skiers rejoiced. Traffic was crazy. The dorm green turned white. Winnie and Melissa trudged through the powder to join Faith and Lauren upstairs in Coleridge Hall, where they drank hot chocolate and watched winter sports on the TV that Lauren had donated to the dorm common room.

While figure skaters spun and leapt, Winnie did sit-ups and talked nonstop. "So I saw Josh yesterday and he was mildly friendly, which I think is the worst possible sign. I mean, if he was still in love with me he would either have ignored me completely or tried to make up. Don't you think? So I figure it's all over and now I'll just totally lose my mind."

"You won't lose your mind," Faith said. She looked out the window and watched the snow flutter down. "Win, there are other reasons to be at college besides Josh. I used to think I had to have a boyfriend." She glanced at Melissa, then cleared her throat. She hadn't been around Melissa much, and didn't know how to react to her ex-boyfriend's current sweetheart.

Melissa smiled and kept her eyes on the TV.

Faith forced herself to keep talking. "I hadn't been without a boyfriend since I was in eighth grade. But now that I've been on my own for a little while, I'm having a better time than I ever did before."

Winnie pounded the floor. "I know, I know. I know there are other things in the world, other fish in the sea, other friends on the clothesline, or whatever the sayings are." Winnie's eyes started to tear up. "I notice that KC didn't show up to join us this morning."

"I called her," Lauren admitted. She sat on the floor next to Winnie, proofing her latest short story. She put the pages down to give Winnie a pat. "KC said she didn't feel well and wanted to go back to sleep."

Melissa nodded. "If she's got the flu I had, she'll be in bed for a few days."

Winnie put her hands over her ears. "I don't want to hear how sick KC is, or how long she'll be in bed. I'm sure KC wouldn't hang out with me now, not even if someone paid her."

"Win, she does have a good reason to be mad at you," Melissa pointed out.

"I know, I know, I know!" Winnie cried. "I know I blew it with Josh. I know I made a mess of things with Travis. I know I did well on my midterms, and I should be happy for that. I know KC deserved what I did to her, and now I deserve having her hate me. I just wish I didn't feel so crazy!"

"Faith is right," Lauren urged. "Just think about classes and forget all this for a while."

"Easy for you to say," Winnie tossed back. "Things with you and Dash are going great now, aren't they?"

Lauren nodded.

"And Mel, you and Brooks made up and are gaga over each other again. Right?"

Melissa gave a slightly embarrassed look at Faith, then nodded.

"Right. So don't give me advice." Winnie lifted her hips in the air and began pedaling. "Travis is leaving tomorrow, but he doesn't want to see me again either, not even to say goodbye. So what am I supposed to do? Change my entire personality overnight? Stop thinking about guys all the time and start studying to become a brain surgeon?"

"Winnie," Faith sighed.

"I know. It's just another mess-up in a huge series of Winnie Gottlieb mess-ups. It's just me. Face it, I'm just Winnie the mess."

"This is all my fault," said Faith.

Winnie frowned. "No, it's not. You're the only one who didn't have anything to do with this."

"Maybe that's what I mean," Faith reasoned. "I wasn't there when you and KC needed me. Not that I regret all the time I spent on *Alice in Wonderland*, but I'm sorry if I wasn't around."

"Yeah," Winnie grumbled. "I'm sorry, too. I'm sorry for everything."

Faith looked out the window again. The snow made the campus look different and it made Faith nervous. No matter what kinds of changes had happened in their freshman year so far, she'd always had KC and Winnie. The three of them had always stuck together. Faith couldn't handle the thought of their trio breaking up.

"It's over," Winnie swore, hugging her knees and looking out at the snow. "KC and I will never be friends again."

Faith glanced around again—at Melissa and the skaters, at Winnie and the snow. "Don't say that. Please."

"Why not? It's true."

Faith didn't know what else to say.

"How are you feeling, KC?"

That same morning, KC could barely lift her head from her pillow. She'd left her window open all night and her room was freezing. She had the shivers. "Marielle. Oh. Hi."

Marielle stood in KC's doorway holding a picnic basket that was decorated with yellow bows. A scarf was wound around her neck and there was a layer of fresh snow on her cashmere coat. "I brought you some things." She took a step into KC's single room and put her presents on the edge of KC's bed.

KC rubbed her eyes. "What time is it?"

"It's almost eleven."

"I must have fallen back asleep."

"I won't stay and bother you. I just wanted to

make sure that you were feeling okay and to drop this off."

"Thanks." KC took the basket and looked inside. Marielle had packed perfume, mints, fashion magazines, and mineral water, plus a canister of the mousse she'd used on KC's hair after Winnie had shoved KC into the pool.

Marielle pointed to the hair mousse. "I thought you'd want some of that mousse, KC, in case you wanted to slick your hair back like that again. Courtney thought you looked stunning. Everyone thought so."

"Really?"

"Really. Maybe I should plan a career in makeovers." Marielle laughed. "Not that you ever needed a makeover, but you know what I mean."

KC unpacked the basket while Marielle fussed about the room, neatening KC's books and closing her window. Marielle's fussing comforted KC and reminded her of her mother. The only time KC really missed her mother was when she got sick.

"Thanks for thinking about me," KC said. "I barely left my room the whole day yesterday. I haven't been feeling very well." She'd been feeling lonely, too. That morning Lauren had called to invite her over to watch TV, but neither Faith nor Winnie had gotten on the line to congratulate her on being crowned freshman princess or even to ask how she was.

Marielle smiled. "I was worried. I could tell that you were getting sick at the formal, and I wanted to make sure you were okay."

"You really did save me, Marielle. I appreciate it."

"I'm glad I happened to be there so I could help."

"Well, you did help."

Marielle shrugged. "What are friends for?"

"Good question," KC muttered under her breath.

"What?"

"Nothing. Forget it."

Marielle went back to the door. "Well, I guess I'll go back to the Tri Beta house and let you get some rest. I'll call you later and see if you need anything else. As soon as you're feeling up to it, maybe we can go shopping or something."

"I'd like that."

Marielle hesitated. "I'm glad that the weirdness between us is over and we're getting to be friends, KC. Especially since I know you'll be a Tri Beta next year. At least I hope so."

KC smiled.

After Marielle had carefully closed KC's door, KC fluffed up her pillow. "I hope so, too," she said to herself. "I guess it's what I want."

But KC wasn't sure what she wanted anymore. She stood up and her head swam. She felt as if she were waterlogged. Even as she rifled through her drawers, she felt woozy. Angry, sad thoughts of Winnie passed in her head, as did thoughts about Warren. KC felt restless and annoyed.

"Oh well, I don't think Warren is going to pursue a serious relationship."

She thought back to Warren's goodnight kiss after the formal. It had been a pleasant but passionless kiss. KC had been relieved when he'd told her that he didn't have time for a heavy relationship because he was too busy making contacts for his modeling career.

KC pulled on sweats, then found her mother's old rain poncho and a pair of tennis shoes. She decided to go out for a walk, even though she was feverish. Anything was better than being cooped up any longer.

The cold air was refreshing. Not many people were out on the snow-covered dorm green. Some of the paths were icy and KC stepped gingerly as she walked by the dining commons, toward Coleridge Hall.

At first she thought of dropping in on Faith, but she suspected that Winnie would still be with her. She took a detour to Coleridge's first floor instead. A few minutes later, she found herself at Peter Dvorsky's room.

"Hi," she whispered, knocking even though his door was open.

Peter looked up. He was at his desk, reading a paperback book. He gave her a questioning look, then a guarded smile.

The snowy light cut across his face. KC wondered how she ever could have taken him for dull or ordinary.

"What's up?" he asked. "How was Winter Formal?"

"Okay." KC stayed in the doorway. "Actually, it was kind of weird. Some of it was great and some of it was terrible. Kind of like my life lately." She rubbed her eyes.

"You look terrible."

"I know."

He smiled. "I heard you won goddess of the harvest, or whatever they call it. I also heard that you and Warren were a stunning couple. Maybe you should marry him and have stunning children."

"Stunning, *boring* children, you mean."

Peter crossed his arms and stared at her. "Is something up with the calendar?"

"No."

"Did you want me to look at one of your papers?"

KC shook her head.

"So why did you come by?"

KC wasn't sure. "I don't know. I wanted to get some air and I just found myself here."

"Interesting. I'll have to get a psych major to interpret."

"No thanks." She leaned against the door frame. "I guess, well, I wanted to apologize for breaking our date."

"Oh." He hadn't taken his eyes off her. "I wish I could say there was no need for your apology. But I'd be lying."

"Are you always so totally honest?" She slapped her hands against her thighs. "Peter, don't hassle me."

Peter stood up and joined her at the door. He stood very close to her and looked into her eyes. "You're the one who came to visit me, KC, not the other way around. Who's hassling whom?"

KC was flustered. Her thoughts went haywire and her heart began beating fast. "What?"

"Why are you here, KC? Just to apologize?"

"I don't know."

He touched her hand. "It seems to me that you don't know a lot of things. Maybe you should start to figure some of them out."

"I will." KC started to leave.

Peter stopped her. "When you do figure things out, KC, let me know."

Their eyes locked.

"You know where to find me," he said.

"I know."

"I'll be here." He smiled. "Not waiting for you. I mean, I'll be here because I live here."

"I know what you mean, Peter."

"Do you, KC?"

KC looked into his eyes until she couldn't take the intensity any longer. She waved goodbye and walked back across the snowy green.

*Here's a sneak preview of* Freshman Loves, *the seventh book in the compelling story of FRESHMAN DORM.*

"F*irst call! Women's four by one hundred meters!*" a voice blared over the University of Springfield stadium loudspeaker.

Melissa McDormand felt a surge of raw energy shoot through her body. Her heart started pumping wildly. After months of training, self-denial, and aching muscles, she was finally going to be put to the test.

Melissa still had several minutes before her race, the eight hundred meters, but she had to begin her warmup right away. She wanted to find a quiet place, but that would be impossible in the crowd. There seemed to be as many people roaming around the track as there were up in the stands.

A glint of gold over by the fence caught Melissa's eye. Standing on tiptoe to see over the crowd, Melissa saw it was the reflection of sunlight on blond curls. Melissa knew those curls—so soft, yet surrounding a ruggedly masculine face, the face of her boyfriend, Brooks Baldwin.

Melissa pushed through the crowd to get closer and saw Brooks lounging against the fence, his solid, well-defined muscles pushing against the fabric of his flannel shirt and faded jeans. As usual, he wore muddy hiking boots. Before Melissa could raise her hand to wave, Brooks caught her eye and smiled.

*"Last call! Women's four by one hundred meters!"* blared the loudspeaker. The jumble of red, purple, gold, green, and white began to organize itself as most runners cleared the track and others unzipped their warmup jackets, heading for the staggered starting lines.

Ignoring them, Melissa closed her eyes and began to breathe deeply, rhythmically. *Inhale, two, three, four. Exhale, two, three, four.* Over and over she repeated the breathing exercise until her muscles relaxed and her mind let go. Then she began to screen out the rest of the world—the track, the officials, the excited crowd, and the other runners.

*Inhale, two, three, four. Exhale, two, three, four.* Melissa knew she could do it. Terry Meeham, the track coach, had drilled the team for months, pushing them through day after day of grueling workouts until they were exhausted. By comparison, running a single race should seem easy. But for Melissa, there was so much at stake that it could never seem easy. Melissa was pre-med *and* on a track scholarship. That put her in a double bind. If she didn't keep up her grades, she'd get kicked off the team, and if she didn't do well in track, she'd get kicked out of school. She had to stay disciplined all the time or everything she'd worked so hard for would vanish.

But for once she wasn't worried. Melissa had never felt so relaxed before a race, so able to shut out doubts and distractions. And she knew why. It was because Brooks was nearby cheering her on.

It was hard to believe she'd given Brooks such a hard time in the beginning. He'd practically had to use a sledgehammer to crack open her hard shell. It wasn't that she hadn't been interested or attracted; she'd just been scared. Scared of getting involved for the first time, scared of letting down her guard, and, most of all, scared of letting anything or anyone distract her from her goals. Melissa still felt that way sometimes, but certainly not right then.

*Inhale, two, three, four. Exhale, two, three, four.* Melissa opened her eyes feeling calm and sure of herself. She was ready.

She dropped forward so she could stretch out

her hamstrings before the race. Then she spread her legs wide and bent over to stretch her spine. From that position, she had a great view of Brooks. He looked just as good upside down as he did right side up.

A pair of purple legs stepped in front of Melissa, blocking her view of Brooks. "Who's the hunk?" asked a voice from above.

Melissa rose and turned around. Her teammate, Caitlin Bruneau, stood before her, her frizzy brown hair pulled back in a ponytail. A junior, Caitlin was the lead middle-distance runner and had taken a special liking to Melissa.

"That's my boyfriend," Melissa said softly.

"Not bad!" Caitlin teased. "Not bad at all! Though I'm surprised you have the time."

"Well, actually I don't," Melissa admitted, "but somehow I seem to find it."

"That's always the way it starts," Caitlin said.

"The way what starts?" asked Melissa.

Caitlin shook her head in mock seriousness. "First a few stolen moments here, some candlelit dinners there, and suddenly you start dreaming of him instead of crossing the finish line."

"Oh, that would never happen to me," Melissa said seriously.

Would it?